A PUZZLE UNDONE

NOLA VEAZIE

ISBN 978-1-64515-535-5 (paperback)
ISBN 978-1-64515-536-2 (digital)

Copyright © 2019 by Nola Veazie

All rights reserved. No part of this publication may be reproduced, distributed, or transmitted in any form or by any means, including photocopying, recording, or other electronic or mechanical methods without the prior written permission of the publisher. For permission requests, solicit the publisher via the address below.

Christian Faith Publishing, Inc.
832 Park Avenue
Meadville, PA 16335
www.christianfaithpublishing.com

Printed in the United States of America

To Jesus Christ my Lord and Savior

God spoke to the people, who were carried into exile from Jerusalem to Babylon, about his thoughts toward them. These words ring true today for those of us who are called by his name.

> For I know the plans I have for you, declares the Lord,
> plans to prosper you and not to harm you, plans to give
> you hope and a future. Then you will call on me and
> come and pray to me, and I will listen to you.
>
> —Jeremiah 29:11

Contents

Part 3

Part 4

Prologue

She!

Who is she? A woman saved by grace, pleasing to the eyes? Or is she a woman with not much to offer? She is old and young in her spirit, trapped and free. She is sad and joyful; the woman is me. You are fearfully and wonderfully made. I formed you in your mother's womb, and your thoughts I know very well, said her maker. I infused the breath of life in you and placed in you my lamp to illuminate the secret places in your heart. Who are you, asked her maker? The world said *she*!

Little does the world know who I really am; little did I know who I was. I can give you the details of my life, the places I've been, the people I've seen. I don't know if I can tell you the reason for my being. I questioned the fairness of my life and waited patiently for a response. In the darkness of night, I hoped for a messenger to come with a special delivery in his hand, but he never came. I concluded in my mind that life isn't always fair. Life may not always be equitable, but its fairness lies in the inequality that makes me who I'm supposed to be. So many stories about me—telling of my disgrace, the man who violated me, the one who left, the mother who rejected me, the sister I wish I could be.

I'm glad life doesn't always end the way it begins; it offers an opportunity for change. If life negated me the opportunity for change, I still would be *she*! This story is for and about every woman. It offers you a chance to water the seed planted in you, a chance to pull the weeds that threaten to choke and kill the seed.

The story of *She* reveals every conceivable feeling you may experience. She is a story about anger, fear, jealousy, anguish, joy, and victory. This is your story, one that highlights all of you—the good parts, the bad parts, the parts you wish you could forget, and the ones you always want to remember. This novel will inspire you to think about your frailty and strength. Most importantly, it will remind you that life is a journey with a purpose.

Part 1

Seeking

Many of you search for something—a mirage that often disappears from view. You search for a shadow that seems to vanish with time and movement, an illusion! You say your quest is to find the story of self. Are you seeking something that seems impossible to find? Looking in the distance for a story untold or was it already told? Maybe your story encompasses every other woman's story. Someone told your story, but no one has ever told your story like this before.

Remember the song "I'm Every Woman"? It spoke of your shared strength and connection to every woman in the world. The song celebrated similarities and uncovered the differences that made you unique. In the similarities, you found your strength and connection; yet the differences enhanced your sense of disconnectedness. Mother told me that everything I need is in me. Unfortunately I felt empty but found what I needed in others. When I began the journey to search for myself, I found my story in someone else.

Most people wish they could see themselves the way they really are. Although deciding who that is may prove more difficult than they think. In their mind's eye, they appear one way. Unfortunately when they look into the eyes of others, the image morphs into someone else—a person they don't recognize. You picture a woman who rises from disappointment to victory, yet others picture her fall from victory into the abyss of disappointment. Your victory depends on the missing pieces of a puzzle—pieces of a puzzle found in someone else's story. The one piece that accounts for your victory is the piece that reveals another person's disappointment.

Do you remember the last time you assembled a puzzle? The joy you experienced when the puzzle was almost complete? You anticipated the revelation of a clear picture, bringing to fruition the reward of your labor. One more piece, and your efforts will be rewarded with the satisfaction that the story is finally complete. The smell of victory quickly turns into the stench of defeat when you realize that you are missing one more piece—a vital one. You cannot complete the puzzle without the last piece!

My client described herself as a puzzle unfinished. Her search for the last piece of the puzzle led her to my office. Imagine coming home from the store, bubbling with excitement, ready to complete your latest masterpiece. Your childlike exuberance takes you back to simpler times. A time when you could do anything you set your mind to do. No matter how complicated it looked, you were confident that you could recreate the picture on the cover. Surprise! When you opened the box, you found that you were missing a key piece of the puzzle. Substituting that piece does not work; forcing it or gluing it on does not work either. The obvious gap left by the missing piece is a constant reminder that you are incomplete. Finding the missing piece to fill the gap becomes your life's quest.

A journey for the missing piece brought my client to the realization that something was amiss. Eve referred to herself in the third person, a noun called *She*! Eve communicated in a way that was intriguing especially in reference to herself. My instinct was to dismiss her as psychotic. However, making a judgment call about my client's sanity was premature. Eve was oriented to person, place, and time—not a picture of someone who was psychotic. I decided to take her on as a client and focused on building rapport. My goal was to listen and observe instead of challenging her peculiar style of communication.

Eve depicted herself as someone who bore the burden of others. She looked at me and said, "I carry the burdens of others like a kangaroo carries her young in her pouch." The name Eve, my client reminded me, was given to the first woman from whom every person had their inception. Eve is also a name that engenders the sins of the world.

Eve was not your run-of-the-mill client. Her very first call to the office signaled that she would challenge everything I learned, everything I knew, my abilities and capabilities. Her call to set up her first appointment was a departure from what I had become accustomed to in my practice. Most clients call and ask for an appointment; they state who referred them, where they found me. For example, some clients state that they found me in the phone book or on the Internet.

Clients often fumble for words to explain why they need an appointment. Reluctantly clients provide their demographic information and often pray for a reason to hang up. Some view the pain of dealing with their situation more excruciating than the pain caused by the actual trauma. Most people know the drill, they negotiate a good time and date to meet with me and the cost for the sessions. Eve simply called and stated with a bit of an attitude, "I need to see someone who knows herself." Without hesitation, she asked the receptionist for available times and dates. When asked by the receptionist for her name, her response was simply, "you can call me She!"

Nothing prepared me for an encounter with this client. I remember sitting in graduate school, attentively listening to Dr. Hill, my professor, talk about establishing rapport and the value of asking open-ended questions. Dr. Hill taught me how to paraphrase and reframe, stating that these techniques would provide clarification regarding direction in counseling. I don't recall him or any of my other instructors saying I would one day encounter a client who would challenge my sensibilities. Nothing prepared me for a meeting with Eve. My psyche was challenged, and I was forced to face my own vulnerabilities.

I sincerely believed that I was prepared, at this point in my life, to handle any situation that presented itself. I was confident because I worked out all my own issues during graduate school. I was prepared to deal with the big T, known as transference in the counseling field. It is not unusual for a client to transfer their unresolved feelings to the therapist. It is also not unusual for a therapist to have countertransference—the transfer of the counselor's feelings about someone else to the client. What I discovered during my tenure with Eve was amazing.

The First Session

Monday afternoons are always busy. Everyone vies for the last appointment of the day, the 6:00-p.m. slot. The last slot in the day minimizes time clients are away from their job. As usual, I reserved a two-hour new-client slot for the first appointment with my client. I needed the extra time to get to know details about her life, family history, and other relevant information especially the reason for coming into therapy. Some clients come in to deal with one thing only to find that it is something entirely different is causing their pain.

I was pleasantly surprised to see a well-coiffed, mild-mannered, and composed woman enter my office. Her designer suit, tailored just for her, laid perfectly on her petite body. The pale-peach single-breasted jacket had pearl-like buttons that brought out the opulence of the suit. Everything about my client spoke to her affluence—the way she walked, the way she carried herself, and even the way she talked. Every word she uttered was carefully measured yet replete with meaning. Eve was skilled at conveying her message using few but carefully chosen words. A single glance from her told a story not necessarily her own. This was not the psychotic client I imagined would meet me for the first time.

Eve sat across from me on a forest-green wingback chair positioned near the door. Her legs crossed at the ankle and her arms delicately placed on her lap reminded me of a debutant. My client quickly scanned the office as if assessing my knowledge of interior design. Her eyes glided, swiftly, across the room, reviewing the way I organized every piece of furniture. Her gaze finally landed on me. Eve quickly scrolled up and down my tailored suit, giving me a hidden nod of approval (as only a woman can do). I believe women have an innate ability to catch the subtlety found in the does-she-look-better-than-me look or the look that says "Is this person worthy of my time?"

"What brings you here?" I asked Eve, waiting for the usual I'm-feeling-depressed answer. Before she could answer, I followed with another question. "Is this your first time in therapy?" The question may have been an attempt to find out if others have failed to help this client, thus, decreasing my anxiety and fear of failure. Eve simply ignored the questions and began to recount her perception of the problem as if she was telling a story.

The self-assured woman instantly became a vulnerable little girl, playing dress up in her mother's clothing. It is amazing to witness the transformation that happens as a client let down the protective walls they erect. What's more amazing is that Eve would let it, down in the first session. "Was it a credit to my counseling skills? Or does it speak to Eve's fortitude?" Dr. D asked herself. She knew that she was not going to get the answer to these questions during the first session. She also knew that Eve's decision to self-disclose during this session had very little to do with her therapeutic aptitude. Nevertheless, Eve's decision to make herself vulnerable gave Dr. D great peace. "She had a sense that she would connect with her and get to the bottom of the problem quickly."

"I could not, for the life of me, describe who I was." Eve said, barely pausing to take a breath before going on with her story. "While seated in my old counselor's office, I came face-to-face with a reality I imagine many women face—not being able to answer the question 'Who am I?' I remembered thinking I'm a married woman, a mother, a friend, a daughter. Every descriptive word about myself connected me to someone else. Although the words linked me to someone, I felt alone and disconnected—adrift like a small boat in a large body of water."

I never heard someone describe their feelings in such a way, Dr. D thought to herself. *This client is a wordsmith, she used words artistically.*

Eve continued telling her story. "Without a palpable connection, I felt as if I was no one. A watermark on someone's document, a page created by the people in my life! The only problem with the picture on the page is—it was slowly disappearing. The vanishing picture would not have bothered me as much if it had not been a picture of me." Eve finally took a breath which gave me enough time to think about the incongruence between the woman that walked into my office and the picture she painted of herself. I cannot imagine anyone thinking of Eve as insignificant. Her presence commanded attention and conveyed her importance in the world. Dr. D was amazed at Eve's ability to tell a story.

Eve proceeded with her story. "My Monday therapeutic sessions were usually uneventful. I talked, my therapist listened, and the session was over." She briefly paused and looked at Dr. D as if she expected her to make a comment, but she didn't. Dr. D noted but continued to listen. "Something tells me that this visit will be different." Eve stated without removing her sight from the story on the pages of her notepad.

"Why do you say that?" Dr. D asked, trying to understand where her client was coming from.

"I get a sense that we have connected on some level. What do you think?" Eve's question caught Dr. D off guard, but she quickly regained her bearing and redirected the client.

"This is not about me nor is it about your connection to me," she stated.

"What is it about?" Eve asked, waiting for her response.

A rhetorical question! I thought long and hard before responding. Dr. D thought to herself. "What do you think it is about?" she asked, hoping her client would not respond with another question.

"Well, I believe it is about connecting me to parts of me I'm not yet familiar with." Eve responded, her words flowing effortlessly off her tongue.

"How do you know that part of you exist?" she asked reluctantly, fearing the first session may have been too intense. Sometimes in therapy, therapists may lose a client if they become too vulnerable too quickly. Fortunately Eve changed the subject which gave her and the therapist time to deal with a more benign subject before tackling deeper emotional issues.

"Can I call you Dr. D?"

"Sure," she responded, still wondering about my client's state of mind. Dr. D's name is Mary Di Angelo, but she figured it was difficult for some people to pronounce her last name; therefore, she allowed her clients to call her Dr. Mary. "Well, most of my clients call me Dr. Mary."

"I'm not like most of your clients." Eve asserted.

"I realize that you are not like any other client I've seen but not unlike them either." Eve became visibly upset but did not respond to the comment. Recognizing that the client appeared upset, Dr. D tried to correct the problem. "I'm sorry if I inferred that you are just like my other clients and not an individual with your own thoughts."

"No big deal" she responded but looked at Dr. D as if she was not really okay with her response.

"Dr. D, where did you go to school?" Eve asked in a matter-of-fact tone as if she and the therapist had not had an uncomfortable exchange earlier.

"I attended the University of California–Davis campus. Does it matter where I went to school?" she asked, feeling a bit insecure.

"No," Eve said without giving it a second thought. I must confess that her questions made me uneasy. I wondered if I could live up to my client's expectations?

As the session progressed, Dr. D's mind began to drift, thinking about her own insecurities. She wondered how prepared she was to deal with this client's issues. Could Eve see right through her? Could Eve tell that she was uncharacteristically nervous about their meeting? She's had wealthy clients before, but Eve seemed different; the only way she can describe the situation is by describing the difference between a meeting with the town's mayor and a meeting with the president of the United States. Although both are important people, one has much more power. Dr. D's mind continued to play tricks on her. She allowed the way her client looked to determine her capacity to provide care.

She supposes many clinicians struggle with some insecurity! Some may even question their own worthiness. She's never felt insecure with a client before. Why should she be insecure? She grew up in a middle-class family—most people would refer to as normal. A two-parent household—her mom stayed home and took care of her, a single child. Her dad was a hardworking man who provided adequately for the family. Most people would say she had the perfect childhood. She attended a good university and graduated cum laude—not an easy feat given all the distractions in college. The therapist continued questioning herself; she carried on an internal conversation even as her client sat before her.

Eve must have noticed that her therapist was lost in her thoughts. "Dr. D, are you okay?"

Jolted back to the room, Dr. D answered, "I'm sorry, I think we are about out of time." She did not know how long she allowed her mind to drift, but it seemed as though she missed the last few seconds of the session. "Shall we meet again next week? Same time, next Monday?"

"Sure," Eve replied, looking a bit disappointed that the session was over.

"Please stop by the receptionist desk before leaving so she can schedule your next appointment."

After the client walked out the door, Dr. D resumed the private conversation with herself. The remainder of that day was a complete blur. She didn't recall what happened during the end of the session or after Eve walked out of my office. She kept thinking about her life, her choices in life, and the people in her life. *Why are some people so lucky*? she thought, knowing that no one would be able to answer this question to her satisfaction, not even herself. Blessings seem to befall people in a random fashion. Some people live a charmed life, receiving everything they ask for. Others struggle constantly, trying to make sense of the chaos in their lives. We all suffer loss, yet some suffer more than their share.

"I'm thankful for the simplicity of my life," Dr. D said to herself, still daydreaming. "I have a wonderful career, a fiancé who loves me very much, and my dog, Casper." Suddenly snapping out of her dreamlike state, she realized that it was time to go home. "Well, thank God it is the end of the day. I think I will go home, lie on the couch, and vegetate while I watch a movie or a soap opera on television. I just hope I don't get any calls tonight. The last time I was on call, I had to deal with a clients-in-crisis marathon. I remember receiving, at least, two emergency calls in one hour." Dr. D said to her receptionist as she walked out the door.

The drive back home was also a blur, maybe because she felt tired. She didn't recall passing by some of her favorite landmarks.

She was amazed by nature's landscape and took in the beauty of each sight. Her mind, like a giant screen, continued playing back the last hour spent with Eve. As a general rule, she doesn't bring the office home with her. The drive between the office and home is her time out. She uses this journey as a time to unwind and express her gratitude for the blessings in life. This drive home felt different; her focus was on solving the mystery called Eve. The therapist was unable to get the new client out of her mind. Although she knew the rules regarding dual relationships (that is having other than a professional relationship with the client), she was unable to stop thinking about her client even though this relationship began in the therapist's mind.

"Home sweet home! Hi, baby, how are you? Have you been a good boy? Mommy will walk you as soon as I take these heels off." Dr. D greeted her dog. Before she could take a much needed but brief rest, the phone rang. "Hello," she said, startled by the loud tone. "Hi, John, I thought you would be on your way here by now." John is Dr. D's wonderful yet unavailable fiancé. "What? So you are saying that you got held up at the office again. Casper and I will be here waiting for you. Do you want me to warm up your dinner? Oh, you are not coming over tonight! I guess I will put the food away. I was hoping we would eat together tonight."

"How was your day?" John asked in a warm and caring tone.

"My day was okay," Dr. D responded with some level of disappointment in her voice. "I saw a real intriguing patient today; working with her will force me to summon every counseling trick in my toolbox. Well, what I mean is…pause, she is a tough one. I'll talk to you about her tomorrow. I love you."

"Casper, are you ready to go bye-bye? I bet you are! I'm sorry, I've been working a lot and not giving you the attention you deserve. I promise I will spend time with you this weekend, having fun in the park. How about a treat after our walk? I got your favorite—delicious doggy treats. Was your day as tough as mine? Sometimes I wish you could answer me. I guess I should not complain. I'm just glad you are a good listener." A thought suddenly came to her mind—*It is amazing how humans can connect with animals, but are often disconnected from other human beings.*

"John and my dog Casper bring such joy in my life." she thought out loud. She doesn't have any kids and very few family members. She's sad because they live three states away. She doesn't socialize much with her colleagues or anyone else for that matter. She guesses listening to people all day makes her want to spend time alone in the comfort of her apartment. Her small two-bedroom space, with its eclectic decor, reflected her personality. A mixture of classic and contemporary furniture, strategically placed, spoke to Dr. D's admiration for old and new—classy and simple.

"Casper, did you enjoy your treat? I know I enjoyed dessert," she responded as if the dog knew exactly what she said. "Shall we take our positions on the couch to watch our favorite channel? Great! Another Danielle Steele movie, I love her stories. Casper, do you enjoy her movies as much as I do? The drama, the suspense, the failures and victories of the protagonists keeps me wanting to see more. Oh, I know, Casper, a little too melodramatic for you." Casper and Dr. D spent the next two hours glued to the television, hanging onto the stars' every word until the end of the movie. "It's getting late, we should go to bed. We need to get up early," she said, nudging Casper to get off the sofa and follow her to the bedroom.

"Oh, my goodness, what time is it? I don't remember falling asleep. The last thing I remembered was getting up off the sofa after watching the movie last night." It was now seven o'clock in the morning. "I've got to call the office and let them know I will be in a little late this morning. Hello, Bertha, what time is my first client's appointment? I'm not going to make it at eight. Who is it? Could you please call Mr. Armstrong and let him know I will be a few minutes late? What time is my appointment with Eve? Nine o'clock? I won't have enough time to get her full family history. Reschedule my 10:00-a.m. client so I can extend my appointment with Eve. I know that follow-up appointments are only a one-hour slot, but I need to gather more information for my intake. Thanks, Bertha, see you when I get there."

☙

"Good morning, Mr. Armstrong, I'm sorry for the delay. The traffic was horrendous. I hope I did not inconvenience you too much. Let's see, where did we end our last session? Oh yes, you were discussing the void left by the death of your wife." Dr. D was barely able to recall a word her client said during that session. All she could think about was her last session with Eve. She inspired a renewed excitement in psychology—Dr. D's chosen profession. She thought to herself, *Lately I have become bored with the usual depressed or anxious client. It is getting more difficult to listen to each client complain about their mundane fights and disagreements with their spouse, their children, their boss, their friends, or someone else. Am I wrong for feeling this way?* She asked herself. I probably sound a little harsh; I must confess, she was glad this conversation was taking place in her head and not with someone else. When did she become resentful about dealing with her client's problems? Did she lose her passion for helping others?

Eve, the new client, brought renewed zest to Dr. Ds practice. She challenged her to delve deeper into her client's lives while exploring the depths of her own life. This call to look deeper at herself and her clients meant that her Monday-morning sessions would never be the same again. For the first time in a long time, she looked forward to the beginning of the week. Once again, she began to feel the exuberance new therapists experience with their first client."

The conversation in her head went on longer than she anticipated. Before she knew it, the session with the client was over. "Well, Mr. Armstrong, our time is up. Please see Bertha to schedule your next appointment. This time let's make it in two weeks instead of our usual weekly session. You are doing fantastic, keep up the good work. By the way, please remember to take your antidepressant medication. They are not time-released and will not stay in your system for an entire month until you take them again." Mr. Armstrong did not like some of the side effects of his medication and often opted not to take them until the symptoms got too bad to handle.

"Uhm, Mr. Armstrong, no more sharing your pills with the cat." Mr. Armstrong was also known to share his medications with his pets.

Mr. Armstrong turned and looked at Dr. D with a sheepish smile and said, "Not even with Pookie?"

"No, Mr. Armstrong, not even with the dog."

"Bertha, I need a few minutes to get caught up on my notes before I see my next client. I've been behind on my documentation since taking on additional work." Dr. D does like seeing her clients, but she hates writing the clinical notes. "Let's see, client seen in therapy session to discuss continued feelings of sadness that began following the death of his wife. This client admits suicidal thinking without any specific plan. Uh! Come on, Mary, concentrate. You know the importance of good notes." Although she looked forward to meeting with Eve, she still dreaded writing clinical notes.

Dr. D found herself very distracted and unable to document the session in a cogent way. Her notes seemed disjointed, and she was having a hard time remembering what Mr. Armstrong said in the session. She doesn't recall ever feeling so anxious about helping a client. Her thoughts were on some of the things Eve shared during that first session. Somehow, they reverberated in her unconscious. She has always been very good with boundaries, not allowing herself to become emotionally involved with any of her clients. For the first time in her career, Dr. Mary Di Angelo could see how a therapist could lose perspective, allowing a client's problems to affect their sense of objectivity.

Have you ever tried to help someone only to become part of the problem? She spent several years in school learning how to avoid that trap only to find herself nearing the edge of the precipice. When you spend a lot of time with someone, you can't help but empathize with them. You can sometimes become less objective, lose perspective, and become one of the actors in the client's drama. She knew that she had not completely lost perspective because she had not, consciously or unconsciously, lost perspective about Eve.

The role of a therapist is not to become a protagonist but to help the client interpret their life script and play the lead rather than the role of a supporting actor. The therapist had to be careful not to take on one of the roles in her client's play thereby losing objectivity. A sign that Dr. D had lost objectivity was her inability to focus on all her clients. Instead she exclusively thought about Eve, the special client she longed to help.

Dr. D continued to ruminate about her client and whether she was capable enough to help Eve. She looked at her watch and noticed that it was almost 9:30. Eve was in the lobby waiting to see her. She took a deep breath, looked at her clinical notes from the week before, and cleared her mind to prepare for her session with Eve. Their first meeting left her both intrigued and apprehensive. She was worried that Eve would not see her as a skilled therapist, able to help her work through the problem that brought her to the office in the first place.

Part 2

Finding

The Second Session

"Bertha, is my 9:30-a.m. client here?" It was almost like asking a rhetorical question because Dr. D knew that Eve was in the lobby; she saw her when she walked the previous client to the door. "Could you please send her to my office? Hello, Eve, how are you?" Dr. D asked.

"I'm well, how are you?" Eve's response sounded very cheerful.

"I'm doing fine, thank you." Dr. D dove right into the session, preventing her client from rambling on about unrelated topics that seemed disconnected from the problem that brought Eve to the office. "Last week we talked about your journey toward self-discovery. You started telling me about the progress you made, or lack thereof, with your previous therapist, but the session ended before you could finish." In an almost predictable Eve fashion, she ignored the comment and took Dr. D on another wild ride.

"Seek and you shall find! Isn't that what the Bible says"? Eve asked and patiently waited for Dr. D's response.

Dr. D shook her head and thought to herself. She was immediately reminded that she would earn every penny she charged this client. "What do you mean?" Dr. D responded, trying to buy time. "I'm not a theologian nor am I very familiar with the Bible." Dr. D said, hoping to redirect the client. Eve simply looked at her but did not say a word. With arms crossed and a stern look on her face, she continued to wait for a response. She seemed irritated but remained poised. It was obvious she did not want Dr. D to ask any more questions; instead, Eve was looking for answers.

"I've been a therapist for many years, and I have had many clients who never found what they sought. On the other hand, I've had clients who did find that one thing they were looking for. I believe that is why they spent time in therapy."

Without skipping a beat, Eve asked, "What about you? Have you found what you are looking for?" In a very professional and therapeutic voice, the therapist reminded Eve that they were not there to discuss her; the purpose of the session was to address the issues that are keeping Eve from enjoying life to its fullest. "We are here for you!"

"Aren't we all here for each other?" Eve responded with a question.

"I guess, in a sense we are. In essence, from a therapeutic standpoint, I'm here for you. Hopefully to help you work through your issues."

"Are you ever there for you?" Eve asked with an honestly inquisitive look on her face.

"I'm not sure what you mean by that question." Dr. D said, hoping to deflect Eve's question.

Eve did not answer the question; instead she answered with a surprising statement. "I recall a time in which I was not emotionally present for the events in my life."

Again, Dr. D interrupted with a question, seeking some clarification. "What do you mean?" As a therapist, she had learned never to assume that she understood her client's perspective.

Eve was not deterred, she continued with her monologue. "In the recesses of my mind, I know that the woman I call She is nothing more than a fragmented picture, an incomplete puzzle." She briefly paused, giving Dr. D an opportunity to take a mental note.

Dr. D thought to herself, *How poetic*. She barely had time to be in awe of Eve's ability with words before being dazzled by another reflection. *The most difficult part of the journey, to find the missing piece, is the starting point.* "Where do you begin the search?" Eve asked as if she desperately sought an answer from Dr. D. "How do you know where to begin when you are not sure where you are?"

Eve's comments did not make a whole lot of sense at the time but was intriguing. "Many people struggle with the same questions,"

Dr. D added. "Who really knows where they are supposed to be at any given time? People know where they want to be! What do you think?" Dr. D asked, praying that she would not answer with another question. Eve did not respond, so the therapist filled the void by asking yet another question. "How do you know when you get there?"

The therapist observed her client's every move as she thought to herself. As she waited for her client to formulate a response to the question, she found herself thinking about a troubling sense of connection to her. Eve was not much different from her; sometimes she neglects to savor each moment and opportunity life presents. Eve interrupted Dr. D's mental ramblings with another question. "Dr. D, is it necessary to find oneself?"

"Do you perceive yourself to be lost?" The therapist asked, buying time once again.

"Not really. Today I feel confident that I'm where I'm supposed to be."

"Do you mean in therapy?" Once again, Dr. D inquired of her client, hoping to get a response that would clarify her statement.

Eve allowed her thoughts to drift away like the windblown waves of the ocean. As Eve's thoughts drifted, Dr. D's thoughts became more singular. She witnessed her client's facial expressions fade but not completely disappear. For one brief moment, she understood what Eve meant by a watermark on someone's document. The watermark is there on the page yet faded into the background. Both the therapist and the client drifted back to the session. "Eve! What are you thinking about?" Dr. D interrupted the brief mental break her and her client took. "I thought I lost you."

Eve appeared temporarily lost, her gaze straight ahead, beyond the office. "What was I saying?"

Dr. D attempted to refresh her client's memory. "You said that you were confident in where you are today."

"Yes," she quickly responded. "I'm here, seeking a solution to life's problems." Eve managed to elude answering the deeper question.

"You never told me what brought you to therapy." Dr. D was not convinced that Eve knew why she sought treatment.

Undeterred, Eve simply responded, "Life!"

"Life happens to all of us," Dr. D countered, "but it does not bring everyone to my office or the office of another therapist. Could you be more specific? What life issues compelled you to seek counseling?"

Eve suddenly changed the subject as if it was taboo. "I'm the middle child you know!" Eve said to her therapist as if being the middle child explained her behavior.

Dr. D did not allow her client to continue deflecting. Instead she challenged her client. "What does that mean?"

Eve opted not to answer the question and did not afford Dr. D the chance to explore her previous comment. Mockingly, Eve asked Dr. D a personal question about her birth order. "What number child are you?" Without giving her a chance to respond, Eve followed up with another statement. "Hopefully you are not the eldest child, they always have issues."

Why did my client ask this question? Did she know something about me? Dr. D seemed paranoid so she tried some self-talk. *All right, Mary, don't allow your client to take you down a rabbit's trail.* The therapist reminded herself that Eve was the client, and the goal was to work on her issues.

It was important at that point to redirect and refocus the session on Eve. Dr. D decided to play detective Columbo. "I'm a bit confused," she stated while scratching her head.

"What are you confused about?" Eve asked with a half-smile on her face. "You're supposed to be the therapist, I'm the client. If anyone should be confused, it should be me." Eve sarcastically responded to her therapist.

Dr. D seem to cower to her client's statement. "I just want to know your thoughts on the subject of birth order. I believe it has a place in therapy, but I'm not sure how it relates to what we were talking about."

"That is why I'm in therapy, so you can help me make sense of things." Eve responded with a pompous attitude. She knew how to elicit a response from Dr. D.

"Touché!" Dr. D responded flippantly. "You are correct—let me rephrase. I don't fully understand why you switched gears in the middle of my question about the events that brought you here."

"Maybe I'm not ready to talk about it."

"I understand, take your time." That exchange brought an end to the discussion about birth order.

Eve had a knack for moving from one subject to the other without bringing closure to the previous discussion.

"Can I tell you a story?"

With some level of resignation, Dr. D acquiesced. "Sure. What is this story about? Or should I say, who is the story about?" Eve came back with another clever response. This client was great with words; she especially had a knack for getting out of tight spots.

"No one you know, or maybe the story is about everyone you know."

Once again, Eve managed to capture the interest of her therapist. "You certainly know how to pull me in to your world yet keep me at a safe distance." Dr. D threw her hand up in the air as a sign of surrender. "You have the floor; I'm all ears." Dr. D watched as Eve accommodated herself in the wingback chair. She took a deep breath and paused for a while. During her pause, Dr. D prepared herself to hear about a horrible story of abuse or neglect related to Eve's past. Instead Eve cleared her throat and waited for a few more seconds before reading an eye-popping story.

"Ready! I'm a little nervous," Eve said in a high-pitched voice.

Dr. D was surprised to hear the high-pitched sound coming from Eve's mouth since her voice was naturally raspy. "Why are you nervous?" Dr. D asked, curious about Eve's sentiment.

"I guess reading in front of someone is not something I'm comfortable with."

"I understand." Dr. D offered her support.

"The story is about a girl I'll call Nadia. I have one request to make before I begin the story."

"What is your request?"

"Please do not interrupt me with questions."

"How do I know what parts of the story apply to your life? Most importantly, how do I get clarification when I am confused about something in the story?" Dr. D's real concern was her desire to find out what parts of the story connected to her client's true self. Perhaps she was still skeptical about the veracity of Eve's story. Eve's answer was brief but clear.

"You don't! When it is time for you to understand, you will. Remember we find ourselves in many stories. You may find me or yourself in one of these stories." Dr. D did not necessarily agree with Eve but nodded and accommodated herself in the chair, ready to listen.

Oblivious to Dr. D's concerns, Eve pulled out a notepad and began to read an interesting story. The first of what would be many stories during her time in counseling. Before she began reading, Eve made an interesting comment regarding the character in her story. "I need you to understand that I am not at liberty to talk about Nadia's identity at this point."

"Why do you feel the need to make such a statement?" Dr. D asked, hoping that her question would force Eve to talk a little more about Nadia.

"Would you like to hear the story?" Eve insisted.

"Well, it is a bit unusual for a client to read a story instead of talking about the reason they sought counseling." Dr. D replied.

"I guess I'm an unusual client."

Aware that she might have offended her client, Dr. D clarified her statement. "I meant your approach to therapy is unusual." Dr. D stumbled over her words as she tried to determine whether she offended Eve with her remark. She was unable to tell if Eve was offended by her remarks. "I apologize if I offended you. That was not my intent. I must say I'm very intrigued by what is written on your notepad." Even as the words came out of her mouth, Dr. D was cognizant that she really felt a loss of control over the session. She felt as if she had allowed Eve to control the session and no longer made decisions regarding what might be best for her client.

Abandonment

Nadia's Song

"The eye-catching array of spring blooms announced the beginning of a beautiful day in May 1985. Each note sung by the birds came together in a harmonious display of musical colors; if you closed your eyes, you could see the hues across the European sky. Sunny Spain was particularly sunny that day with a slight crisp chill in the air that crystallized the musical notes from the birds and the colors from the flower garden. Looking back, it was as if the chill captured the colors and sounds like the matting that frames a painting. Nadia recalls the beauty of that day and summarized it as the kind of day you capture in your mind like a picture you pass on from generation to generation.

"As in the calm before the storm, she felt the buildup of anticipation and tension that came down like a shadow over the perfect day. Like in the eye of a hurricane, the calm was felt for a brief moment and then gave way to the disturbing force of nature known as anger. It seemed like out of the blue, a four-inch blade suddenly pierced the soft colors and replaced them with the deep red color of blood. In one fell swoop, anger turned Nadia's song into a sad story. No longer were the birds singing, and the rays from the sun stopped shining and drizzling gold tones on the flowers and fairy dust on people passing by.

"One thoughtless move turned the light of day into the blackest night. *Who turned off the light?* The question appeared in her mind like a ghost lurking, waiting to materialize one day. Anger jumped out of the shadows and took center stage without an invitation. This is Nadia's story—one shared by many others who, like her, allowed anger to reign for a moment. The Word of God says that weeping may endure for a night, but joy comes in the morning. Some mornings, it seems the reverse is true, weeping endures a lifetime along with the darkness of the night.

"What can I say about my story?" she whispered. "I was married at a young age and entertained all the same fantasies most young married women do. I wanted two children, a loving and successful husband, and a career. I never gave much thought to any particular vocation. I just wanted to be successful at whatever I did. I was very much like any other young working mom, juggling the responsibilities of work, motherhood, and being a wife. Unlike most other young wives and mothers, I carried a tomb full of the dead bones of repressed anger.

"My anger lay dormant for years, peaking to the surface once in a while when someone or something provoked it, like bait coaxing it out of the dark waters. Repressed anger…Hmmm… Sounds like some rare disorder found in a psychology book, but it is not. 'Repressed anger is simply anger that is locked in the closet of your mind, not easily accessible or so I thought,' said Nadia. Something that is hidden for so long seems strange when it appears. Anger was no stranger to me yet that day, I hardly recognized it. I remember the pain tumbling out of my heart, wrapped in this familiar stranger called anger.

"My lifelong goal was to succeed in the workplace. I could hardly identify the energy that seemingly fueled my drive, but it kept me striving, so I did not rock the boat. The same energy also kept me from reaching deeper depths of intimacy in my relationship. It energized me just enough to maintain the status quo but not enough to want to go to that place of oneness. I never questioned my inability to go to that place, but I knew that something had to give. I never thought that something would be me." Pausing for a second, Eve looked past the therapist as if she were transparent, as if reviewing the videotape that played over and over in her head.

Suddenly Eve snapped out of her daze and continued the story. "Nadia asserted, my life was good for a while, but I can't pinpoint the moment things changed." After reflecting for a short period of time, she blurted out, "No, I do know when things changed. Things changed and seemed different when I became the throwaway child. What do I mean by the throwaway child? The throwaway child is the vulnerable child in all of us who is left unattended or pushed to the side by the people who professes to love her. In my case, it was the child who was left by her daddy (Eve recounted this part of the story in a childlike tone as she comforted herself with a hug). You would think that all these years later, I would not need a daddy, but all children need a father." Eve paused for a second, but it seemed as though it was an eternity as her sad eyes drifted to the floor.

Dr. D reflected as she listened to Eve's story. She was pleasantly surprised by the poetic way in which the story cascaded off Eve's tongue yet somewhat disturbed by the words coming off the pages of her notebook. This woman, Nadia, must have been in great pain. As Eve read the story, she tried without success to imagine the pain the character must have felt. Was it simply a character, or was Eve recounting her own story? She was a little confused by the incongruence between Eve's affect and the words coming from her mouth. She can't imagine someone experiencing such disappointment and not shedding a tear as they recall their pain.

Eve continued to recount the story. "A throwaway child!"

This phrase hit her like a brick, so she interrupted Eve. "Why did Nadia feel that way?" Dr. D asked, knowing that she may not get a response from her client—at least not one that was satisfying. The therapist's hope was to find out if Nadia was Eve. "Dr. D, remember the request I made before I began the story?"

"I do remember your request, Eve," Dr. D responded. "I'm confused by your reaction to the story. You seem so disconnected from the emotional pain in it."

"What do you mean?" Eve seemed surprised.

"Well, hearing Nadia's story makes me feel sad, and the sadness reflects on my face." Unfortunately Dr. D was unsuccessful in her attempts to help Eve connect to her emotions. Eve continued with the story.

"This isn't about my husband! I think it has more to do with my dad but let's talk about my husband. John began to drift away from me and move toward drugs and other women. His emotional exodus soon turned into a physical one, leaving me feeling abandoned and helpless. The more I think about it, the more he reminds me of my father, but that is another story. I remember clearly the day I saw him with that other woman. She represented something more than another woman—I just did not know it at the time. I don't know if anyone else can relate to the feelings she represented in my mind, a void left by my father, abandonment! I guess we can call this woman Abandonment."

Again sadness like a mist covered Eve's eyes, making it difficult to see into them. She paused before looking at her notes and continued as if telling her own story. "My husband John and Abandonment, his new mistress, began to consume my every thought. I often found myself thinking, *What are they doing? Where is he? What is her hold on him*? The question I should have asked were the following, what is her hold on me? I did not realize she kept a strong grip on one side while anger (my partner) held on tight on the other side. The force of the two pulling me in opposite directions, at times, almost tore me apart. What drives a person to this point? Nadia asked as if someone would appear and answer the question.

"I finally succumbed to the force exerted by abandonment and anger. On that faithful day, my husband, John, was getting ready to go out, I don't remember where. That sunny spring day turned into a chilling and bloody afternoon—a day I will never forget as long as I live. I tried to stop John. I begged him, 'Please stay, don't leave me.' The vacant look in his eyes reinforced the thought in my head that I was a throwaway child, one who was easily discarded. Suddenly my partner (anger) spoke up and said, 'Take control, don't let his mistress (abandonment) win this battle,' and I snapped." Eve stopped reading and looked at Dr. D, her eyes beckoning her input.

"What are you thinking?" Dr. D asked with a quizzical look on her face.

"You know, Dr. D, Nadia did not even remember holding the knife in her hands or seeing her husband on the floor, bleeding to death."

"I guess anger blinds people," Dr. D responded. Eve did not respond immediately, so the therapist filled the void with nervous chatter. "Anger often takes us to a place we do not want to go."

Finally Eve spoke up and said, "Yes, it turned Nadia into a person she hardly recognized." The statement seemed to energize Eve, and she proceeded to tell the story. "But the Word of God says that he will restore the years the locust has eaten. In this case, the locust was my anger. God's faithfulness filtered through the anger and allowed a ray of light to reach those dark and broken places in my heart. I finally realized that I had the power of forgiveness. I had the power to regulate the heat of anger and release myself from the ties of abandonment. God's mercy and grace did not allow John to die nor did it allow me to spend the rest of my life in jail. Instead God taught me to accept his forgiveness and give it to others."

"That was a very interesting and sad story. Is it real or fiction?"

"I rather not discuss that with you at this time," Eve's response was short but clearly expressed some emotional connection to the story.

Dr. D wondered about Eve's fierce protection of Nadia's story. She sensed that they were getting into unchartered territory. She did not want to push, yet she needed to know more about the protagonist in the story. She decided to use a little reverse psychology by talking about the impact the story had on her. "Eve, I don't know about you, but that story really made me sad."

"I guess it can impact people that way." Eve responded casually as Dr. D tried to detect a hint of sadness or other emotions.

The therapist decided not to continue to press her client for an explanation. Instead she pursued a different strategy to get additional information about Nadia. She concentrated on the obvious religious overtones in the story in an effort to bait Eve into divulging her connection to Nadia. "I did not know you were religious," Dr. D said, hoping that Eve would take the bait.

"I'm spiritual, not religious," Eve responded with indignation as if Dr. D was questioning her religious belief.

"Did I say something wrong?" Dr. D wanted to ensure her client did not misconstrue her statement.

However, Eve did not seem receptive to the feeble apology. "I believe you should understand the difference between religion and spirituality."

"I suppose you will educate me," Dr. D responded.

"You are the therapist, I expect you to be more sensitive to the spiritual leanings of your clients."

Almost immediately, Dr. D became aware of her own mind chatter. *Is this client saying that I am not showing empathy or sensitivity to her needs? Mary, remember she is the client.* Dr. D recognized that she had become emotionally involved with her client and might be losing objectivity.

Dr. D chose not to continue deliberating the notion of religion with her client; instead she refocused the conversation. "Eve, tell me about Nadia."

"What can I say about her that I did not say when I read her story?"

"Why do you suppose she tried killing her husband?"

"I don't believe she tried to kill her husband. I think she was trying to say something."

"What was she trying to say?"

"Perhaps she was trying to communicate her loneliness." For the first time since Eve walked in to her office, Dr. D clearly saw a veil of sadness replace the confidence her client wore like a mask.

"How did Nadia communicate her loneliness?" Dr. D's question seemed self-directed—a veiled attempt to address her own sense of loneliness.

"She spoke through her actions. In fact, I believe her message speaks to many women who are watermarks on someone's page."

"A watermark?" Dr. D asked.

"Yes, a watermark." Her client's response expressed an emotional depth that extended to previously untouched areas in Dr. D's heart.

"I could not discern if the story was about Nadia, Eve, or someone else." Dr. D was confident, however, that it would reveal a connection to her client's inner conflict. "Does this story depict a past event or does it predict the future?" Dr. D tried once again to penetrate the thick wall Eve erected. She got no response, so she tried again. "Have you ever felt like a watermark?"

"Of course I have! I told you that during our first session."

"I see. The good thing about a watermark is, although faded, it still exists." Dr. D had barely finished her statement before Eve explained that it is better to be here and faded than not to exist at all.

Her reasoning was astounding. Unlike clients who are consumed by their problems, Eve appeared to have insight into the issues she struggled with. Many of her clients lack insight into their problems and therefore, exercise poor judgment. It was difficult to assess Eve's judgment because she was so guarded. Up until this point, she was careful not to disclose anything that showed vulnerability.

Although Dr. D was fascinated by Eve's insight, she was unable to stop thinking about Nadia's story. Once again, she pressed Eve for more information. "How does Nadia's story relate to yours?"

"Do you think it relates to mine?" Eve had a knack for answering a question with another one.

"I don't know," Dr. D responded. "You have not told me much about yourself."

"My father, like Nadia's, was MIA in many ways, at least emotionally."

"MIA?"

"You know, missing in action."

"Yes, I get it. For some reason, I thought your father was around."

"In many ways, he was." Eve responded before taking a deep breath and pondering her next move.

Finally Eve seemed ready to talk about her connection to the story. "Where was he?" Dr. D asked with some trepidation, trying not to spook her client.

"He was around but not there."

"Strange response. What do you mean around but not there? How did his absence affect your life?" Dr. D realized she did not give her client time to process and answer the first question before following up with another one—not a good therapeutic approach. Fortunately Dr. D's approach did not seem to affect Eve.

"I'm here, how do you suppose it affected me?" Dr. D was still unable to make sense of her client's problem, but the therapy session was almost over.

"Where did the time go?" Dr. D said out loud, indicating the end of the session. "Two hours hardly seem enough." Two hours had gone by; however, Dr. D was still confused about the reason for her client's visit to her office.

"No amount of time is enough to dissect someone's life," Eve asserted.

"I agree with you. Unfortunately, I have several lives to dissect." Dr. D responded half-jokingly, resisting the pull to address her comments. "Let's leave something to talk about during our next meeting." Dr. D ended the session with Eve; however, she was left with an irresistible urge to continue exploring Nadia's life.

Dr. D found herself once more in her head, thinking about what transpired earlier. Today's therapy session left her wondering what it might feel like to grow up without a father. Would her life have been any different? She found herself engaged in a very unfruitful one-way conversation. It was reminiscent of a one-man ping-pong match, and the ball was in her court. The drive home seemed longer than usual, but she continued torturing herself with questions about Nadia or was it about Eve? Secretly she began to feel consumed by Eve's story. She felt as if her life was on a collision course with Eve's."

"Finally! Home sweet home. I'm exhausted. I think I'll snuggle with Casper since John is not coming over tonight. I am a little disappointed that he is not coming over. Having John in my life sure is wonderful. What would I do without him?" Dr. D continued the conversation with the dog, ignoring her feelings of disappointment. "Poor Eve, she must be awfully lonely without someone special in her life." Long pause. "For some reason, the apartment feels empty tonight. Casper, where are you? You know I don't like to play hide and go seek." Dr. D was suddenly overcome by an unfamiliar feeling. "I don't recognize this feeling I'm experiencing. I wonder...Is this what lonely feels like?" She did not allow the feeling to linger very long. Instead she immediately distracted herself by playing with the dog.

"There you are, Casper! Were you hiding from me?" Although she tried to distract herself, Dr. D continued to experience a deep loneliness she was unable to shake. "Casper, what do you suppose is this strange sensation I'm experiencing? I know, you are probably thinking it is the pizza I had earlier." People, including therapists, try to avoid negative feelings that cause them to feel vulnerable. "I think I'm beginning to overidentify with my client. This only happens to inexperienced therapists, but I'm a veteran. I don't understand why Eve's story affected me this way. Loneliness is not a feeling I've struggled with in the past. Why am I experiencing these feelings?" Concerned that she might be overwhelmed by the relatively new feeling, she began to rationalize. "Maybe I just need a vacation. I have not gone on one in three years."

Dr. D had a propensity to compartmentalize and to deflect—hazards of the job. She was always able to use Casper and television as escape mechanisms. "Here we are again, Casper. What should we watch on TV tonight?" She looked down at the dog, waiting for an answer. "I agree, a Lifetime movie sounds good. I don't think I am ready for another love story. I am not sure I can deal with this tonight." Her thoughts wandered for a second before continuing her monologue.

"Who wants to watch other people make out when you are alone? Casper, do you think Eve was right when she said that nighttime is the loneliest time? Well, she did say that the night was like a black canvas upon which the pain of loneliness is often painted. I think her assessment might be a little dramatic. What do you think?" Her countenance was sad, but she refused to allow the sadness to control her. The helper was in need of help; she looked at Casper and said jokingly, "How much do I owe you for the session? I owe you $320? Casper, you are an expensive therapist." She snuggled with her dog and watched movies until she fell asleep.

"What time is it?" She awoke in a panic only to find that it was still nighttime. "Casper, why didn't you wake me up? Let's see, what do I have on my schedule for tomorrow? I have a full load. Note to self—remember to call Mr. Armstrong to follow up on his belief that his dead wife has been breaking into the house and cooking breakfast. I think I may send Mr. Armstrong for a medication evaluation. He seems to be getting worse since his daughter got married and moved out the house.

"Casper, was that the phone? Yes, it is," Dr. D answered her question. "I knew I heard the phone ring. Hi, John, how are you? I was just writing myself a reminder to refer one of my patients for a medication evaluation. I thought this patient was doing well, but he suddenly began to deteriorate emotionally. Yes, there has been a recent change in his life." John often acted as her sounding board and at other times, he was her personal consultant.

"What's changed?"

"The most recent change in his life was his daughter's wedding. His daughter moved back in with him when his wife died, but she recently got married and moved out. The prospect of really being alone must be terrifying to him. You are such a big help, thank you, John."

Dr. D paused for a second before continuing her conversation with John. "I have another patient you might be able to help me with. She is a new client, but I have not been able to figure out what she is doing in therapy. John! Are you there? I thought I lost the connection. I was saying that my new client is an enigma. Why? We have had two sessions, and I still don't know why I'm seeing her. She seems very open and shares a lot of information, yet she tells very little about herself. I realize it has only been two sessions but with managed care, we may only have a few more.

"How have I handled a situation like this in the past? I don't think I'm exaggerating when I say I have not seen anyone like this patient before. The client (she could not mention her name due to client confidentiality) is very skilled at telling a story that may or may not be hers or contain parts of her story. My challenge is to figure out which part of the story is hers and which part is not.

"Once again, thanks for the free consultation. I'm a little tired, I think I will go to bed, it's late. John, will you be over tomorrow?" She asked, longing to enjoy his company. The desire for companionship was very new to Dr. D. Her busy lifestyle did not allow time to think about her loneliness or the desire to spend time with others. No one would describe Dr. D as a very emotional person, certainly not a touchy-feely kind of person. Her relationship with John exposed a side of her she was unfamiliar with. In fact, she could not say with certainty that she ever allowed herself or another person to experience her vulnerability. She wondered if John was responsible for accessing buried feelings or perhaps, it was a result of the unusual relationship forged with her client. Either way, those feelings caught her off guard. Her loneliness floated to the surface and took center stage. She recalled feeling unfamiliar emotions, the likes of which she had never experienced, not before Eve's initial visit to her office. She wondered if it was a good thing to be less afraid to explore more vulnerable areas of her life, buried emotions that kept her from undergoing change. She became less afraid to confront those dark areas of her life—areas that prominently displayed a "Do Not Disturb" sign.

"Tomorrow is a new day and a new opportunity for discovery. I wonder what I will discover about myself?" The therapist who spent her life's work helping others find their happy place finally gave herself permission to experience a small piece of the happy pie. The days were no longer passing her by. She no longer felt empty and adrift in the world. She took a long look at herself in the bathroom mirror as she put on her makeup. "I don't recall ever spending this much time examining myself. I suppose we all have an Eve in our lives—someone who forces us to look deeper inside ourselves and face the truth."

Unfortunately truth is not always objective. Truth is often someone else's view of what transpired. People pass it down from one generation to the next, adding their feelings and interpretation of the truth. What some people consider truth is simply information afforded them by a certain time and space in history. Dr. D thought about her client and her belief about truth; she considered Eve's perception of truth to be vaguely familiar.

Anger

The Third Session: Victoria's Secret

"Bertha, is my client here? Please send her in, thank you. Good morning, Eve, how are you today?" Dr. D greeted her client with enthusiasm. She seemed refreshed and ready to go toe to toe with her client.

"What is your definition of anger?" Eve asked abruptly, overshadowing Dr. D's initial confidence.

"Maybe we should start the session by addressing Nadia's story," Dr. D asserted.

Eve insisted that her question was related to Nadia's story and thus, repeated the question. "What is your definition of anger?"

"Well, I would describe anger as a negative buildup of energy, caused by an internal or external—" Dr. D was unable to finish the sentence before being interrupted by her patient.

"Blah, blah, blah, I don't want to hear all that psychobabble."

"How do you feel when you are angry?"

She felt frustrated by what she perceived to be her client's attempt to evade questions about Nadia. "This is our third session. We should really focus on the issues that brought you here, especially the story about Nadia," she said in as calm demeanor, hoping not to offend her client.

"Don't worry, Dr. D. We will have plenty of time to deal with Nadia."

After some thought, Dr. D responded in a way that would hopefully elicit insight from her client. "How much time will we have to deal with, Eve?" She asked in a non-threatening way. Once more, her client gave one of her unusual replies.

"We have a lifetime!"

"I have another story for you, Dr. D," Eve said in a playful way.

"Is it about Nadia?" the therapist asked, hoping to finally discuss her concerns about Nadia's story.

"No," Eve replied without hesitation. "This story is about a woman I call Victoria."

"Why do you call her Victoria if that is not her name?"

Eve had a well-thought-out response. "Victoria implies victory over this woman's struggles."

"Is that right? What struggles did she achieve victory over?"

"Listen to the story, maybe you will learn about Victoria's secret." Eve's response was not meant to be mean; she simply wanted her therapist to hear and understand the story.

Eve pulled out the familiar notepad on which she had scribbled another amazing story. Although Dr. D had become increasingly frustrated by her client's ability to evade any attempt to refocus her on the problems that brought her in to therapy, she was able to pique Dr. D's interest every time she read one of her stories. "You may start reading whenever you are ready," Dr. D said reluctantly. Dr. D also reminded Eve in a firm voice, "I would like to discuss my concerns when you are finished reading."

Eve sat up straight in the wingback chair that was strategically placed near the door. Dr. D noticed that Eve did not begin to read the story immediately; instead she took a long (maybe five seconds) look at her therapist. She would dare say that Eve looked through her before reading the following words, "The word *venom* conjures many images, all related to poison and death. Victoria's story is one that could have ended in emotional and spiritual death but as the Word of God professes—the end of a thing is better than the beginning. Victoria likened this chapter of her life to a journey into a bed of venom, a pit full of destructive snakes waiting to inject her with their paralyzing and deadly substance. I was injected!" Eve exclaimed in a low-pitch tone. "I was injected with the type of venom that is far more insidious than the venom of a snake. The type of venom that slowly infects every fiber of your being until it takes full control of all that is good and pure in you—the venom of anger!

"I became cognizant of my inner struggle when I realized that my fairy-tale marriage never existed. The marriage that was supposed to be a fantasy was instead a nightmare—one I was unable to awake from. Denial became a comforter but was replaced by the venom of anger I embraced as a friend. At my lowest point, my anger moved up in rank until it replaced God in my life. My anger consumed every thought and permeated every fiber of my being. Who is this person in the mirror? I hardly recognized myself anymore. It was as if this feeling that took over me changed the way I looked and felt."

As Eve recounted the story, a noticeable change came over her affect. The anger she spoke about was reflected on her countenance. Her soft face became hardened and appeared to age before the therapist. For a moment, Dr. D thought maybe she had stepped into the twilight zone. The petite, sweet Eve was no longer before her; Eve experienced a metamorphosis of sorts. Dr. D was unsure whether she should interrupt the story to address what she witnessed or just let it flow. Instead she decided to allow Eve to continue telling the story.

Her client proceeded with the story, speaking as if she had read her mind. "It was as if my soul was hardened and covered the goodness in me, but it did not stop me from trying to love." Eve recounted the story with sadness in her eyes. "The venom of anger, injected in me, caused me much pain. The only way I found relief was to inflict that pain on my husband."

I found what she said very interesting but will not comment on it, Dr. D thought to herself. Eve proceeded with the story. "The rejection I felt was similar to what I experienced in grade school. The kids made fun of me because of my strong Southern accent, my appearance, and sense of style. All the feelings from years past rushed back, and I suddenly felt like a yoyo on a string, spinning out of control only to be rewrapped in anger.

"Have you ever loved someone with your eyes wide open?" As she was about to interject some thoughts, Eve cut her off and continued with the story. "Anger either keeps you from loving, or it closes your eyes to the truth—the truth about yourself! Coming face-to-face with your pain is not easy but even harder is facing the angry person you've become. The reflection you see in the mirror is a person who can no longer acknowledge the good in someone else. The mirror reflects a person who sees only bad things about others and criticizes them."

As Eve neared the end of the story, Dr. D remembered thinking that this one was not as graphic as the last one. She also remembered how upset Eve became when she interrupted her during the last story, so she chose to wait until she finished before asking questions. "The dawning of a new day is here!" Eve continued with the story. "I've escaped the bed of venom and chosen to take the seat of forgiveness. I learned that I was fearfully and wonderfully made and that God's thoughts were on me before my beginning. It is a great revelation to know that I have a comforter who gives me a sense of security. When I'm afraid, he loves me even when I'm unlovable. This comforter reflects the true me when I'm blinded by my anger."

"I noticed that all your stories contain religious overtones."

"I have not shared all my stories with you yet," Eve said, flashing her signature smile.

"You are correct. The two stories you have shared so far are filled with faith-based language." Dr. D said with a hint of sarcasm.

"What do you think about Victoria?" Eve asked her as if she told the story for her benefit.

She wondered how Victoria's story connected to Eve's story; so she asked. "How does Victoria's story convey your feelings about relationships?"

"I'm not sure I can answer that question. In fact, I don't think I fully understand the question." As Dr. D pondered the best way to rephrase the question, Eve interrupted with an observation. "I do know that victory in relationships comes by achieving victory over our own emotions. What do you think?"

"Fantastic!" Dr. D exclaimed, amazed at her client's insight. Perhaps Eve was finally willing to embrace the therapeutic process. "Does your statement imply that you are in therapy to address the negative emotions that affect your relationships?"

"Perhaps!" Eve responded without further explanation. Following the exchange, both women paused for a few seconds—possibly contemplating the implications of Victoria's story on each of their lives. Eve finally broke the silence with another insightful comment. "It is on the road to escape your biggest fear that you meet your destiny face-to-face."

"You are on a roll today. What is your biggest fear?" Dr. D asked, hoping to gain more insight into Eve's life.

"Losing myself to someone else."

"Wow, that is deep." Finally Eve opened up enough to let her therapist take a peek inside her world.

Dr. D took advantage of the slight opening and asked about the significance of the stories. "Let's talk about some of the victories and defeats you have experienced in your relationships."

"What would you like to know, Dr. D?" Eve responded with a bit of sass.

"Was it a relationship that brought you into therapy?"

"Yes, a relationship with myself."

"What do you mean?" Dr. D asked, hoping that this time, Eve would actually talk about herself.

The poised, small-framed woman who walked into the therapist's office a couple of weeks ago suddenly reemerged, but she was different. Dr. D could not put her finger on the difference; how had the client changed? Somehow the person that walked into her office a few sessions ago disappeared, giving way to this more vulnerable person. This version of Eve wore a pale-yellow suit with a chiffon blouse, an A-line skirt with pleats at the bottom, and sling-back white shoes. She wore her hair loosely curled and combed back. Eve sat in the wingback chair with her legs crossed at the ankle. There was one major difference. This time, the debutant allowed Dr. D to go beyond the insurmountable wall she had erected during the last session.

Eve took a long deep breath and readjusted her skirt. She nervously fidgeted with her clothes, trying to delay the unavoidable. Finally she spoke. "I was married for fifteen years to a man whose name I don't wish to reveal at this time."

"I am surprised. You never mentioned that you were married," Dr. D said with a hint of amazement in her voice.

"You never asked," Eve sarcastically responded.

"You are right. It must have been a tough marriage."

"Why do you say that?"

The therapist searched for the right words to answer her client. "Well, people often conceal painful areas of their lives."

Eve pondered Dr. D's assertions before answering. "The marriage was not always toxic. We were very much in love in the beginning." A veil-like sadness descended over Eve's face; at the same time, a wider opening appeared in the protective wall. A crack in her tough exterior. "I'm unsure when the marriage moved from a well-watered garden to the toxic dump it became."

"Those are very strong words you used to describe the relationship. I am surprised by the level of your emotions especially because you have been aloof the past sessions."

Undeterred by her therapist's last statement, Eve proceeded to discuss the topic of love in marriage. "Have you ever been in love?" Eve asked the question, not necessarily expecting a response because she continued talking. "I was madly in love with my husband. We shared everything—our thoughts, our dreams, and our emotions, at least that is what I believed…" Eve hesitated but continued to share her story. "It is hard to place yourself in someone's arms for safekeeping."

"Ha!" An unintelligible word uttered by Dr. D interrupted Eve's word picture regarding the state of her marriage. "I am sorry, Eve, but I would like to get a better sense of what you mean. Explain what you meant by placing yourself in someone's arm for safekeeping?"

Eve graciously clarified her statement. "Trusting someone you love with who you are. Isn't that what we are supposed to do in our relationship?" Eve gave Dr. D the impression she might not have made the right choice by getting married. It was not anything she said, just a feeling that came over the therapist. "Maybe I gave away too much of my power," Eve continued.

"Does it feel that way? How much power would you say you gave away?" Dr. D's line of questions were intended to promote reflection, but she feared the questions may have overwhelmed the patient.

Eve became silent after Dr. D's questions; she appeared to be deep in thought. It took a few minutes before she responded to the questions. "Trust has a deeper meaning than we understand. When you trust someone, you give them permission to watch over the physical, emotional, and spiritual parts of you." She paused and then said, "When you are unable to do so, if I'm having a bad day, or I am hurting emotionally, I need to trust that my partner will be a sentinel (watchman)—one who alerts me when an intruder tries to assail me."

Dr. D chimed in. "Unless the intruder is your partner."

"Yes, of course, unless the intruder is my partner." Eve repeated, agreeing with Dr. D. "The world is filled with people and situations that threaten to harm me. I rely on the people I love to watch my back and protect me from the dangers I'm not aware of. I place complete confidence in those people and when they fail me, I consider them no longer trustworthy."

"Wow. How fair is it to place that much responsibility on one person?" Dr. D asked. She hoped the light bulb would light up. "Eve, I hope you understand that others cannot take responsibility for your feelings. In fact, they cannot always protect you."

"I don't know how fair it is, but that is what I need."

"That is an honest response," Dr. D replied to Eve's statement. Her goal was to help her client realize that others cannot be responsible for their feelings. "Eve, you cannot always rely on someone else for emotional protection."

Eve ignored the comment and continued sharing, her gaze fixed on the floor. "My husband was supposed to be the one person I could go to for refuge, but he turned out to be the person I ran from." Eve was finally exploring the pain she previously avoided. Even though her thinking errors kept her in a victim stance, she seemed ready to face the truth about her pain.

"How does your story compare to Nadia's?" Dr. D doggedly seized the opportunity to examine Nadia's story and dig deeper into Eve's past. She may have acted prematurely, though, because Eve immediately shut down.

The sophisticated woman who walked into Dr. D's office only a few weeks before was becoming a mere mortal before the therapist's eyes. Dr. D reflected on the first time she met Eve; she appeared to transcend the problems written in her journal. Yet here she was, a woman in pain like most of us. The therapist wondered out loud. "Have you ever been intimidated by the polished CEO or the woman next-door with a husband and two kids who is able to multitask? She brings home the bacon, fries it up in a pan, and never lets hubby forget he is a man. She rises above the problems other women experience without becoming overwhelmed by them."

"What!" Eve exclaimed. "I am not sure what you are talking about. Are you talking in general or talking about me?" Eve asked.

Dr. D realized that she had allowed her thoughts to escape her mind. "I am sorry. I wasn't aware that I spoke out loud. I was talking about the woman who seems untouched by the difficulties of this world. You know, she seems perfect, able to handle everything. The reality is, she does not exist!"

"You are right. That woman is a figment of our imaginations," Eve responded but re-evaluated her statement. "Why can she do it all, Dr. D? Who decides the limits we should place on anyone?"

"You are right Eve. We shouldn't place limits on another's life."

Sensing they were getting offtrack, the therapist decided to refocus her attention on Eve's affect. Her vacant eyes, saddened by life's experiences, appeared to look into an unattainable future. "What are you thinking?" Dr. D asked, hoping that Eve would continue to talk about her marriage or perhaps gain the courage to talk about Nadia. Dr. D was not sure why Nadia's story was of so much interest to her. Somehow she felt if she could get Eve to talk about Nadia, she would reveal more about herself.

"I'm thinking about my life's journey. We come into to the world for a short time, and then we leave it. The dash between the date of our birth and the date of our death is the journey."

"I am not sure what you mean?" Perhaps Dr. D understood but felt torn between the need to continue to explore the previous conversation and her desire to understand Eve's state of mind.

"Let me explain." Eve proceeded to give an example. "You know, the day you are born and the day you die—May 12, 1960 to May 13, 2002. The dash, small as it may be, reflects someone's entire life's journey. What they did from the time they came into this world until their exit through death. The dash reflects the people they touched with their God-given gifts, the people they neglected, their victories, failures, and most importantly what they did with what was given to them."

Intrigued by Eve's explanation, Dr. D silently hung onto each word. Finally she broke her silence. "I see, that makes a lot of sense."

Following a long pause, Dr. D spoke up again. "Eve, how would you describe the dash that represents your life?"

"The verdict is still out. I have not completed my journey." Eve refused to elaborate further. It was obvious she would not allow her therapist back into her world, at least not right now. The one-hour session was almost done; Dr. D decided not to pursue a response. She figured that by allowing her client to process the information from today's session, she might be more open to talk about Nadia next week. At least that was the plan.

"Our time is up," Dr. D said reluctantly. "Please see Bertha on your way out to schedule our next appointment." Eve did not complain nor did she push back about ending the session prematurely. The conversation left an indelible mark on both therapist and client.

After Eve left her office, Dr. D sat on the wingback chair and wondered about the dash in her own life. *What does the dash in my life represent?* She started another mental dialogue that often left her emotionally drained. *I've touched many lives in my career as a counselor. How many lives have I touched as a human being? This might require some vulnerability on my part—I'm not sure I can allow that.* The mental ping-pong started right after Eve exited her office. Thoughts swirled in her head so fast, it made her head spin. "I am getting a headache." Dr. D said to herself. However, she did not allow the pain in her head to take away the elation she felt over the progress Eve made in the session.

"Focus, you need to get your notes done." Dr. D started writing her clinical notes, making sure she did not leave out any details. She was still reveling in the progress she'd made with Eve when Bertha reminded her that her next client was waiting.

"Hello, Mr. Armstrong, how are you? Please come in and have a seat."

The time with Mr. Armstrong went by so quickly, Dr. D did not realize the session was over. She spent the entire session thinking about her meeting with Eve. She was unable to recall a word Mr. Armstrong said because her mind was preoccupied. Dr. D felt energized by the prospect of finally addressing Eve's life and the lives of each character in her stories.

Enmeshment, the inability to see where one person ends and the other begins! Dr. D began to jot down some notes in her client's file. Her notes took on a different tone; they seemed more personal this time.

> I knew I had to get back on the subject of Eve's marriage. I was also aware that it may be difficult to get her to talk about the relationship with her husband. Although Eve told me that she was married, I was still surprised to hear her speak about the marital discord. During the beginning sessions, she managed to keep the focus away from most of the details of her life including her marriage.

Dr. D suspected that Eve had a less than functional relationship with her husband; however, her initial presentation led the therapist to believe that the dysfunction was mainly due to her dissatisfaction with her life.

The therapist's focus on her client's life seemed almost obsessive. The remainder of the day was filled by her thoughts about the session with Eve. However, there was a part of Dr. D that questioned her own existence. "What have I done, thus far, with the dash in my life?"

The question spoke to the unfinished business in the therapist's own life. "When my obituary is read, what will it say? I wonder if I would be proud of the life being read aloud for the world to hear. I was not sure what my gifts were." Eve had a way with words which caused Dr. D to think about her own life—the significance of the dash in her personal journey.

Tough session, Dr. D thought to herself as she walked out of her office to head home. She barely recalled the drive home but there she was, at the front door of her apartment. She put the key in the door and stood there for a few seconds before entering, but a loud bark snapped her out of a deep trance. A beautiful curly-haired poodle jumped on her with excitement, eager to get some attention.

"Hi, Casper, how are you?" Dr. D suddenly became aware that she had been interacting less and less with her dog. "I know you've missed me, but I've been very busy at the office. Get your leash, we are going for a walk in the park." As she walked the dog, she noticed people passing by and thought about the dashes that told a story about their time on earth. "People walk by each other not realizing that some of our dashes might intersect at some point in time. We fail to slow down and see that the dash in our lives may very well impact the dash in someone else's life," she thought out loud as she walked her dog and watched people pass by. The funny thing was, Dr. D didn't seem to mind if anyone thought she was crazy because she was talking to herself. She felt a sense of freedom she had never experienced before.

Dr. D decided to end their walk early. "I need to stop the flow of thoughts and give my mind a rest." She was aware of the obsessive nature of her thoughts and desire to explore dormant issues in her life. "Come on, buddy, let's go home and grab our spot on the sofa. Guess what we are doing tonight?"

If Casper could talk, he would say, "Let me guess!" Dr. D continued talking to Casper. "We are watching another movie on the Lifetime channel. Popcorn?" she asked, excited about the prospect of submerging herself in another story. Dr. D spent another night immersed in the life of the characters in movies she loved watching. Perhaps the goal was to escape her own life.

As time went by, she felt less and less satisfied with escaping reality by burying herself in her work or in her favorite Lifetime movies.

She became more aware of her daily routine and the lack of outside connection to others; Dr. D seldom deviated from the comfort of her predictable life. She thought to herself, *What would happen if I go for a walk after work instead of coming home first?* The initial thought of change elicited feelings of panic; in fact, thinking about doing something different was stressful. She made up a million excuses in her head about why she needed to go straight home. The almost endless barrage of thoughts assailed her mind.

"I needed to walk the dog."

"What if something happens while we are out?"

"John may want to come over for dinner."

"What if I miss one of my favorite movies?"

In the middle of the rapid-word fire, Dr. D came face-to-face with the realization that the real reason she did not want to change was fear. "If I allowed myself to live rather than exist, would I be all right?" This question gave her pause but did not deter the endless cycle of questions in her head.

"Casper, did you know that many people pretend to live but merely exist? The fear of failure deters many from fulfilling their destiny in this world. The fear of walking outside of the boundaries other people set up for them limits their ability to complete the picture on the puzzle box. I wonder if I am doing the same."

A question popped in her head seemingly without permission. "What if I allowed myself to color outside the margins? I seldom entertained such thoughts, but Eve's stories opened my mind to new ideas." Dr. D felt as though she just jumped out of a plane (a perfectly functioning one) and allowed herself to soar like a bird. "Now I know why the caged bird sings," she jokingly said to herself. "The thought of escaping his prison and experience the beauty not far out of reach brings him joy." For the first time in her life, Dr. D experienced feelings of true freedom. Feelings similar to a person recently released from prison; a person experiencing the outside world again for the first time in a long time.

Finally it seemed the mental exercise was over. Then she began to anticipate her next session with Eve. Dr. D felt torn between the desire to find out everything about her patient and the awareness that she was losing herself in her work. She had become so consumed by Eve's stories, she neglected other clients; her thought about the stories occupied her mind. Even her relationship with John became less important, taking a back seat to her thoughts about Eve. Her dog, Casper, endured countless nights listening to ramblings about her newfound emotional freedom. The Lifetime movie channel became less important; she no longer buried herself in the stories. Instead Dr. D began toying with the idea of living out loud. She became tired of living in the shadows of fear, scared to uncover the missing piece of the puzzle.

With each passing session, Dr. D realized that the relationship with Eve would soon come to an end. She wondered if she would revert to her old self or would go on to search for the missing piece of her own puzzle. She dreaded the thought of living this life without making her mark in the world. The biggest fear was to look back over her journey only to find that the dash was a faded one. Not having an impact in life was as scary as facing the demons in recesses of her mind

Rage

The Fourth Session: Wanda's Story

Generally by the fourth session, the client reports feeling comfortable with the process and the therapist. Because of managed care, most therapists begin to talk about termination during the final sessions. This session signaled the impending end of the therapeutic alliance. Unless a client can afford to pay, wrapping up the session becomes imminent.

"Bertha, could you please find out if Eve's insurance will give us additional time? I think we are almost out of allotted time." Afraid that her client may not be able to continue in therapy, Dr. D contemplated Eve's journey—how much work could they do in the short time left? What would she do after her insurance ran out? Would she stay and complete the process? Would she abandon the quest for the missing piece of the puzzle? These and other questions about Eve consumed her thoughts.

Dr. D's anxiety level rose as she allowed thoughts to race through her mind. *What am I doing? I need to stop.*

"Bertha, is my client here?" Dr. D took a deep breath, gathered her notepad, and positioned herself to receive her client. "Hello, Eve, how are you?" She appeared calm and collected as she greeted her client.

Eve, on the other hand, did not waste any time; she jumped right into the session. "Dr. D, did you figure out what the dash in your life will say about you?"

Her question left the therapist a bit off balance, but Dr. D did not allow the question to rattle her entirely. "As much as I would like to discuss the dash in my life, Eve, you are paying me to help you figure out your life." Dr. D did not let on that she had been thinking about the subject matter since their last session.

Without further discussion, Eve began recounting a story about a woman she met during her travels around the United States. Eve started the story by saying, "Wanda compared herself to a wild animal, cornered one too many times. The backwoods of Louisiana was the breeding grounds for more than reptiles. The small town was also the safe haven for an entire family of predators who lured Wanda into the swamp. Her husband and his family were members of the KKK. Chet, his mother, and two brothers were proud card-carrying members of the Klan."

Dr. D thought to herself that Eve was very consistent; she started each session by asking a question before introducing a story about a different woman. *By this time, I learned to listen attentively to the story without interrupting her. I figured I might glean something from her stories especially the ones I believed pertained to my client's life,* Dr. D thought to herself. *Every story we tell reveals some truth about our own lives.*

Eve went on with her story, despite the look of concern on her therapist's face. "Wanda did not stand a chance in her new family's home. Her husband, Chet, directed his rage not only at people who were different, he also directed it at his wife."

Against her better judgment, Dr. D interrupted Eve to ask what she was doing in the backwoods of Louisiana. "Eve, why were you in the backwoods of Louisiana?"

"Searching for the missing piece of the puzzle," Eve responded.

I honestly was not surprised by her response. I learned to expect the unexpected from this client, Dr. D thought to herself.

Eve continued narrating Wanda's story. "Wanda came from a middle-class family. She was no dummy, just in love like many other twenty-something-year-olds. Wanda fell in love with a fast-talking man who was five years her senior.

"Wanda was an average looking woman but by the time I came in contact with her, the years had taken its toll." Eve sighed before going on with the story. "I met Wanda while seated in a bus terminal."

"Why were you in a bus terminal?" Dr. D asked, knowing that her client would come up with a very interesting story.

"I too was fleeing my past!" Eve responded with sadness in her eyes. She then pulled out her writing pad, and the words began to leap off the pages as if they were alive.

Eve continued telling the story but this time, in the first person. "I left my parent's home to start my happily ever after with Chet. Someone neglected to tell me that love stories don't always have a happy ending. My husband's tall, muscular frame leaned over to open my door, and I just melted into the front seat of his 1965 Chevy."

Red flag. How can Eve know someone who was in her twenties back in 1965? Dr. D thought to herself but chose not to bring it up.

"I felt like a princess being carried off in my carriage to my king's palace. I don't remember what song was playing on the A-track because I was mesmerized by Chet's deep-blue eyes and wavy blond hair. By the way, Dr. D, by the time I met Wanda, she was much older than me."

It was as if Eve read her therapists thoughts and answered her question. *Is my client clairvoyant*? Dr. D asked herself. *How did she know what was on my mind*?

Eve did not notice the curious look on Dr. D's face; she went on with the story while her therapist grappled with questions about the timeframe. "The nine-hour drive from my parents' home to my husband's parents was amazing. We laughed, we talked, and we planned our future together. Anyone who's ever been in love would understand my delusional state of mind. Chet was so attentive and kind, I felt safe moving so far away from my family. I did not know my husband's family. Chet rarely talked about them, and I was so in love I did not ask many questions. I knew that his mother's name was Sarah and his father was Bruce, but that was the extent of my knowledge about the family.

"Welcome to Manny, Louisiana, population 450—my introduction to hell. Manny was a small town with a big secret. We drove up to a tiny wood-framed house painted in white with blue trim with a sign that read 'The Bradshaw's.' Before we could get out of the car, we were greeted by Mr. and Mrs. Bradshaw, Chet's parents. He was a tall robust-looking man, and she was small-framed and frail-looking. Both Chet's parents were in their late fifties but looked much older. I remember thinking, maybe they worked hard all their lives and it took a toll on them."

"Hi, Mr. and Mrs. Bradshaw, I'm Wanda. To my surprise, Mr. Bradshaw responded (in broken English and a drawl), 'Sun, you don good fo youself.' Mrs. Bradshaw, Mama Elaine, as she was referred to, rushed over and hugged me. 'Good meeting, ya gal,' she said with the same accent. I noticed more people emerging from the tiny little house. It reminded me of a clown car in the circus. You see one clown after another coming out of a miniature car. The Bradshaw household, I would soon find out, was no laughing matter.

"'Come see, Mama,' Bill (Chet's younger brother) yelled. 'You come see,' yelled back Mama Elaine. 'Your brother's new wife is here.' That first introduction was the last time I felt welcome and loved. Our honeymoon was spent in a room at Chet's parents' house which became our permanent residence. It did not take very long for my happily ever after to evaporate.

"The Bradshaw family depended on the welfare system, and Mr. Bradshaw was on disability. They blamed their lack of work opportunity on those immigrants from across the border and often used the N word to refer to African Americans. The level of hate emanating from the Bradshaw's home was worse than living in a toxic dump near Three Mile Island. The first time I spoke up against this hatred became my first encounter with Chet's fist. He knocked me to the ground where I lay in shock. I could not believe this was my knight in shining armor, the very prince who drove me in my princess carriage not many days before.

"I pulled myself up as I wiped the blood from my mouth while the family stood and watched. My disbelief was compounded by what Mama Elaine said, 'Wanda, you can't go making Chet mad.'

Her statement was a harder blow than the one her son inflicted on me. I knew better than to talk back. Instead I plotted my escape from the Bradshaw's house. How could I tell my parents what I was experiencing? I felt ashamed and lonely. There was another emotion welling up inside me—anger.

"Chet quickly rushed over to me and apologized. 'I'm sorry, baby, but you shouldn't say things that make me mad.' Still in a daze, I allowed the family to convince me, in spite of my better judgment, that I was wrong. 'I will run you a bath and get you cleaned up,' Chet said as if I had done this to myself. It felt so good not to hear the yelling and screaming. I just went with the flow."

Dr. D interrupted Eve to find out more about this latest character. "How do you know so much about Wanda?"

"When you spend as much time searching for self, as I did, you also find out about others."

"What do you mean?" Dr. D asked, anticipating the same colorful response as before. She wondered if Eve was making up these elaborate stories. How was she privy to the intimate details about the lives of so many women?

"Dr. D, you don't get out much, do you? If you open yourself to others, they will share their lives with you." How ironic—the client counseling the therapist about becoming a better listener.

Eve's statement gave pause to Dr. D and made her reflect on her own journey. *I spend so much time listening to my clients' problems that I tune the world out once I leave the office. I wonder if I neglected listening to my own thoughts*. Dr. D soon tuned back in to her client. "Eve, what feelings does Wanda's story bring up for you?" Dr. D's question provided an opportunity to disconnect from her feelings and refocus on her client

"I feel sad that Wanda had to experience the pain of abuse," Eve responded with congruency in her affect.

"How does Wanda's experience relate to your life?" Dr. D expected Eve to ignore the question or simply dance around it.

"I certainly can identify with the pain caused by disappointment in someone you love. I cannot say that I have experienced the physical pain of abuse. However, I'm familiar with the emotional pain." Eve's level of disclosure was extremely surprising. The therapist listened as her client peeled back each layer of her life, revealing a quiet, inner strength.

Eve returned to her story, noticeable drained from talking about her emotional connection to Wanda's story. "Wanda was not very different from you or me," Eve said to the therapist with great sadness in her eyes before she continued to read Wanda's words. "The remainder of the night was difficult for Wanda. Her thoughts about the events that transpired earlier kept her awake and afraid." Dr. D noticed that Eve was now telling the story from the third person's perspective. She wondered if Eve changed from the first person to the third person when the story did not connect as much to her own story. She decided not to address the issue because it may not be as important.

"'Wanda, wake up, it is seven in the morning,' Chet screamed in her ear. Her new husband was uncouth as they said in that part of the South. 'I have to go help Daddy with some work in town.' *This is my opportunity to get away from this nightmare*, Wanda thought but feared the consequences. Unfortunately the bad dream would last another year and take a tremendous toll on Wanda's body before she finally mustered the courage to leave.

"November 1966, one year after riding into town with her knight in shining armor, Wanda drove away without Chet. Wanda was left with a broken body and scarred emotions inflicted by the rage that consumed her husband. She no longer looked like the young, pretty girl who drove up to the Bradshaw's with her husband. Aged by both the emotional and physical scars, it was hard to recognize her.

"Her exodus from the tiny town of Manny, Louisiana, was an opportunity to reclaim the important parts of herself."

Sensing the story coming to an end, Dr. D interrupted with another question about Wanda. "What made Wanda finally leave Chet?"

"The last straw was a broken jaw and a few broken ribs, but nothing compared to her broken spirit. Rage," Eve pointed out, "acts like a shredder that tears apart the beautiful writing of one's life. The intensity of rage renders the spirit unrecognizable. Wanda refused to be further complicit in tearing apart the essence of who she really was. Her body and emotions would eventually heal. She was not sure her soul could, so she left. Wanda's story highlighted the inner strength some people possess during dark times."

Dr. D thought about her client's ability to summon that inner strength. "In what ways have you been shredded by rage?" The therapist asked, sensing that this might be the appropriate time to discuss the pain that led Eve to her office.

"My heart bears the scars of many broken promises, lost opportunities, unfulfilled dreams, and many disappointments."

"I sense that you are intimately familiar with a life shredded by rage," Dr. D said to Eve, still wondering about her story.

"My life certainly reflects the scars left as a result of being shredded by anger." Eve continued to be evasive in her answers, but Dr. D had become more skilled at retrieving the truth about her client's feelings.

"How is your husband similar to Chet?" Dr. D recognized that Eve's storytelling contained some parts of Eve's story. She continued to ask questions, hoping to get to the heart of the problem.

Eve nervously repositioned herself on the wingback chair and started twirling her hair with her right hand. "I don't think my husband is anything like Chet," Eve replied in a low voice, glancing out of the window over Dr. D's shoulder.

"How is he, Eve?" Another question in an attempt not to lose momentum.

"I think our time together has come to an end." Eve abruptly ended the session without further discussion.

"I learned that people open up and talk about their pain when they are emotionally ready to do so. I won't push you to talk about something you obviously are not ready to talk about." The session ended without further discussion about Wanda; although, Dr. D desperately wanted to make a connection between Wanda's story and Eve's.

"Should I make an appointment for next week?" Eve asked as she gathered her things.

"Yes, please let the receptionist know that I want to see you back next week for an hour appointment. Great session, Eve. I look forward to discussing your relationship with your husband."

Eve hurried out of the office without responding to the statement.

"I think I might be on to something. Why else would Eve rush out of my office so quickly?" Dr. D said out loud as if she wanted Eve to hear her. Hoping to keep momentum and make some headway during the next session, Dr. D called the receptionist and asked her to schedule a two-hour appointment. Perhaps a longer session might afford her an opportunity to connect with her client on an even deeper, emotional level.

Fear

The Fifth Session: Nicolette's Story

During the last session, Dr. D and Eve made great strides. Both were pleased with the progress. Although Eve shared more than she anticipated. "Hello, Eve, you look great." Dr. D's greeting was warm and friendly; she hoped to have a great session with Eve. Her client walked into the office wearing a pleated brown skirt and a yellow chiffon blouse with tear-shaped pearl buttons. The skirt was long which was unusual for Eve. She looked sad but maintained her usual composure.

"Good morning, Dr. D, how are you?" They exchanged pleasantries but got right to business. Eve appeared preoccupied as she fumbled to take out her notepad. Dr. D observed her client intently but chose not to comment about her demeanor or recap the last session. Wanda's story was still fresh in her mind. She wondered about Eve's connection to Wanda but figured she would let her client guide this session.

After a few seconds fumbling to find her notepad, Eve pulled it from the bottom of her large purse. She didn't ask a question or preface the story. She simply began reading. "I was far too young to experience the things I saw, heard, and felt. Fear! That is the emotion that overtakes you when you can't find a place to hide."

Dr. D watched every move her client made, every gesture as she allowed those words to roll off her tongue without a hint of emotion, but she dared not interrupt her. "I turned over and saw seven men, twice my age, lying beside me, all waiting their turn to savor my innocence. They took the last lifesaver I clung to—hope! Their touch on my body felt like I was being scorched by the desert sun that dried the last drop of morning dew from my body.

"I was trapped in an apartment as life went on outside, and no one was aware of my existence—no one except the seven men and the woman who kidnapped and placed me there. Samantha, my captor, knew I was only twelve years old, but the only thing she could think of was the amount of money my curly blond hair and striking looks would bring her. I was 5'8" with strawberry blond hair, green eyes, and smooth skin, I was quite the looker.

"As I lay there, I thought about the two girls I ran from the group home with and wondered where they were. We were all separated after running for thirty minutes. We figured this strategy would help us ditch the cops. I sure wish I had stayed with them because there is safety in numbers. I remember meeting the girls while we were locked up in juvenile hall. We were young and still innocent. Everyone told me I looked so much older than I was, but I was naive. I reveled in the idea of looking eighteen instead of twelve. As I lay trapped in Samantha's apartment, however, I wished the seven men beside me could see that I was only a twelve-year-old child.

"Like most of the other girls I met in juvenile hall, the hall as we referred to it, I had become very promiscuous. I always craved attention. I looked for love in all the wrong places and from all the wrong people. That day, however, I looked for an escape from my captors. I wanted to escape the pain of my past and the horror I believed would be my future if I was unable to leave.

"How did I meet Samantha? I was on the run from my third group home, hoping my parents would come looking for me like parents do in the movies. I walked the streets of the tiny town where the group home was located, hoping that the staff would call my mom and dad. I fantasized about my parents jumping in their car and driving nine hours to the small town I now lived in to rescue me. When they got there, they would hug me and tell me that they made a big mistake by placing me in a group home. I always felt if I was bad enough, the group-home staff would send me back home with my parents. No such luck. Unfortunately anytime I ran from one group home, I was sent to juvenile hall and then another group home.

"This latest absence without leave or AWOL, as the staff referred to an unauthorized absence, landed me in the arms of my captor. Samantha was a forty-year-old woman who lured young women to her apartment with the promise of saving them from the streets, from going to juvenile hall, or being placed in a group home. I jumped from the frying pan right into the fire! This experience eclipsed any pain I experience in my past.

"When did my nightmare begin? The year 1982 was a great year for punk rock, spiked hair, and me. I had the privilege of making my appearance in this world. Shortly after my introduction, I was placed in a foster home because my biological mother was unable to care for me. Mom was strung out on drugs, and my biological father was nowhere to be found. Turned out, Mom had to make a choice between me or her drugs, and I was on the losing end. The couple who saved me from Mom, and later adopted me, took good care of me initially. My adoptive dad's love, however, seemed to change when nature began to take its course. As I got older and my body began its transformation to womanhood, my adoptive father took notice, and my adoptive mother looked the other way.

"My body matured by leaps and bounds ahead of my mind. At the age of eleven, I looked more like a sixteen-year-old teenage girl with more than her share of blessings. I jumped from a child's body right into the body of an adult woman. How interesting, all I wanted to do was play with my Barbie dolls and my Easy-Bake-Oven. My adoptive mom always said, 'Nikki you have to wear a bra for support.' The only support I needed back then was hers. I craved to have my mom's arms around me, reassuring me that everything would be okay.

"My biological mother's drinking and drugging habits during her pregnancy left me with even bigger problems than the need for foster placement. I was what the medical community and others referred to as a drug baby, afflicted with mental health and other developmental problems. The drugs did not affect my physical development which became my saving grace. I believe this body kept a roof over my head and afforded me some luxuries. You may think the luxuries I'm talking about are jewelry or toys, but I'm talking about food and clothing.

"Mr. and Mrs. Anderson, my adoptive parents, were model citizens in their community. They were church-going folks who volunteered their time to help those less fortunate like myself. In addition to church activities, you could always find Mrs. Anderson at every PTA meeting and bake sale, lending her services to make the lives of others better. You may wonder if she had time to take care of six children. Well, between her four biological children, my brother and me, she did not have much time. Mr. Anderson, a real-estate broker, often pitched in and took care of us children.

"The Anderson's were a great and loving couple! Have you ever wondered what happens when some folks take off their Sunday clothing and nice hats? Not every person who claims to be the citizen of the year does the right thing. My foster father, for example, lived one life in public and another behind the picket fence. The white picket fence surrounding the house not only kept intruders from coming in, it also kept secrets from getting out.

"The summer of 1993 was unforgettable not because it was filled with great memories. Mom and Dad woke us kids up early as it was the custom on Sunday mornings. Everyone had their assigned seat at the table where we sat to eat our traditional Sunday breakfast. I can still smell the hotcakes, sausages, and eggs. That particular Sunday morning turned out to be the bleakest day of the summer. I told my parents that I wasn't feeling very good. I had severe stomach pains from something I ate the day before, so the family went on to church without me. My dad decided to come back home early to take care of me. He took care of me all right, he introduced me to some of life's lessons I was not prepared or mature enough to deal with.

"During my first encounter with the secret rituals grownups practice behind closed doors, I just lay quietly. I recalled looking up at the ceiling wondering what would happen next."

It was apparent Dr. D was troubled by the injustice done to Nikki. She twisted and turned in her seat, wringing her hands as her breathing became shallower. Dr. D took advantage of a lull in the story to stop the narrative. "Can we take a break?" Eve paused to take a breath, creating an uncomfortable moment of silence. "This story is hard to hear, but I know it is an important story to tell. I felt a compulsion to stop you when you spoke about Nikki's trauma."

Eve did not respond to the statement; in fact, it did not seem like she heard Dr. D because she kept talking. Dr. D continued listening with disgust as Eve told Nicolette's story. She felt hopeless and helpless as she listened to the horror this young girl must have felt. It was interesting to watch the therapist cringe while the client did not seem bothered by the unimaginable details of the story.

"My foster dad got up when he was finished and walked out the door as if nothing had happened. I remembered thinking the water was not hot enough to burn off the shame that covered my body. A steady stream of thoughts went through my head, but I can't tell you what they were. Why was this happening to me? Ironically I felt special because he chose me over one of his own daughters. Equal to the stream of thoughts through my head were the string of emotions parading through my heart.

"'Hi, Mom, how was church?' I asked without raising my head to look her or any of my siblings in the eye. Since that day, I don't recall looking anyone else in the eye. I feared that someone would read my thoughts and discover my shameful secret. It's very complicated because along with the shame, I felt a sense of pride. I became my dad's special little girl, I've never played that role before. Unfortunately I became one of those China dolls people enjoy and place back on the shelf.

"It is interesting that Mom never noticed that I was a different person. I was not the little girl she left that morning. It's amazing how one's life can change so quickly. It does not take a lifetime to become experienced in life—it only takes one traumatic experience. At seven thirty that morning, I was an innocent little girl. By noon, my innocence was gone. I became more aware of my body and the benefits it could afford me. Thereafter, I held the secret that gave me the power to get what I wanted.

"Dad continued his undercover charade, pretending to be a loving husband and father, all the while stealing the innocence from the child he vowed to protect. Each visitation from my dad took another part of me. Ironically he thought he gave me something invaluable. He gave himself permission to take something precious from me—all under the guise of preparing me to deal with the men that would later come into my life. The many men that followed further contributed to my destruction.

"What would my real mom and dad think about Mr. Anderson? I wondered if they knew my secret. Would they regret choosing drugs instead of me? Unfortunately I would never hear the answer to those questions. In fact, I never heard the answers to many of my questions. As I lay surrounded by the seven men finishing what Mr. Anderson started, I realized that I had even more questions. This time, they were about my future.

"Here I was, face-to-face with the future I feared. How did I get from my foster father's bed to Samantha's? Another parent figure destroying rather than protecting my innocence. Samantha, I later found out, was the female equivalent of a pimp. The way she made money and got her drugs was prostituting young girls who ran from their homes. Not all the girls were runaways. Some looked like the all-American-girl next-door, except these girls were looking for excitement. The girls ranged in ages from twelve to nineteen, and most of them, like me, were seeking something to fill the void. Some were drug users who supported their habit by indenturing themselves to Samantha."

Eve stopped abruptly as if interrupted by an external force or perhaps her thoughts. She slowly lowered her writing pad and started to cry. "I don't understand why bad things happen to innocent people. Nicolette's story is recreated a dozen times in the lives of so many girls. I wish I could save them all." Eve became clearly upset and decided to take a short break.

"You can't save everyone," Dr. D said to Eve, hoping to minimize her obvious distress. This was her opportunity to re-engage her client on an emotional level. She took advantage of Eve's moment of vulnerability to talk about her feelings, hoping it would lead to the discussion about her marriage. "I noticed that a sense of hopelessness came over you as you read Nicolette's story."

Eve lifted her head as she listened to Dr. D and then replied, "Her story reminds me that terrible things are sometimes visited upon the innocent."

"Yes, Eve," Dr. D responded. "It does rain on the just and the unjust alike. Sometimes unjust people seem to have an umbrella that protects them from the rain while innocent people get soaked." Dr. D's response sounded dark and hopeless, but it didn't seem to deter her patient.

Eve picked up her writing pad and continued to read Nicolette's story; a single tear drop glided down her cheek, but she did not bother to wipe it. "I closed my eyes and wished I could fly away. I envisioned myself back in my mother's womb, protected from the awful reality I found myself experiencing. I knew I could not physically escape what was happening, so I mentally checked out. When it was over, I lay down on the floor and cried for the innocent girl I left in my tiny little town. The little girl the Anderson's adopted into their home was gone forever.

"Samantha tried to reassure me by telling me that everything would be just fine. All I had to do was take the tiny pills she held in her hands. It would make me relax. I don't remember much after taking those pills. I woke up out of my stupor several days later, not feeling any better than I did when I first took the pills. I noticed that each time I took those pills and smoked the funny cigarettes she gave me, it became easier to do what she wanted me to.

"I never thought I would do the things my biological parents did! I swore never to use drugs because I did not want to be like them. I did not want to follow in the footsteps of my sperm donor and the woman who carried me. My greatest fear became my reality. I found myself resenting them even more than before. They brought me into this world only to abandon me to the wolves.

"The week I spent with Samantha felt like a lifetime. Every day I opened my eyes, it felt as if I was in a never-ending nightmare. At least when I closed my eyes and slept, I escaped the cruelty of my reality. Fear—not necessarily the absence of courage. What I lacked was the strength to summon that inner voice that would say to me, 'You are worthy.' A voice that would give me the green flag to escape a future I refused to accept as my own."

Another pause in the story gave Dr. D an opportunity to interject her thoughts about the character. "Nicolette is a very brave girl," she exclaimed, hoping to re-engage Eve in more self-disclosure. Dr. D was also aware that they were approaching the final number of counseling sessions; Eve's insurance would only pay for a few more sessions.

While Dr. D was preoccupied by thoughts of losing her client, Eve gazed out the window behind Dr. D's desk before she exclaimed, "Nicolette's bravery sprang from her fear! My greatest victories came during times of great fear."

Dr. D didn't understand the comment; everything inside her wanted to scream, "That doesn't seem right." *How can bravery spring from fear*? she thought to herself but did not have time to comment because Eve picked up the notebook and continued to read Nicolette's story.

"The voice that gave me the green flag to escape did not spring from within, it was the voice of one of the employees from the group home. Brenda kept an eye out for me even during her off time. She saw me and another minor walking with Samantha and called out my name. I was afraid to run from Samantha. But this time, I felt smart fear, the kind that makes you run from danger, not toward it.

"My fear kept me trapped in Samantha's clutches, using drugs to escape the harsh reality I faced. Mom and Dad were never coming to get me. A little before being placed in the group home, I reported Dad (Mr. Anderson) to the authorities. I was the one locked up while the Andersons continued to live in their make-believe world. I never saw or heard from them again. I no longer wanted to live in fear, so I decided to live. Escaping my past is not going to lead me to my future. I realize that the road I was on led to my parent's past."

Eve put down the tablet and turned her eyes to a painting that hung on the office wall. "There are so many roads on this journey. It is sometimes difficult to figure out which one to take."

"Are you talking about Nicolette or about yourself?" Dr. D asked, secretly hoping that Eve was talking about herself. Maybe Eve would summon the courage to talk about her journey, but she did not say a word. Her gaze seemed transfixed on the painting as if she did not hear the questions. Dr. D repeated the question which irritated her client and abruptly ended the conversation.

"Dr. D, I think it is time to end the session." The therapist reluctantly agreed and asked her to stop by the receptionist's desk and ask for a follow-up appointment in one week. Letting Eve off the hook was the best thing the therapist could have done at that point. Her demeanor changed, and she sounded more relaxed. "That sounds great, Dr. D," Eve replied without protesting.

Following the session, Dr. D sat on her chair and stared at the wall while formulating a plan in her mind. *I must confess, Nicolette's story left me shaken. I wonder if I should contact the authorities to ensure this young girl is okay? But what would I tell them? Was the story real? Where did this rape take place? Eve never mentioned the city or state nor did she mention Nicolette's last name.* Therapists are mandated reporters; like teachers, they are required to report child abuse/neglect and elder abuse. Dr. D continued her internal conversation. *I feel helpless. On one hand, I have to protect my client's confidentiality. On the other hand, I'm required to report a crime against a minor.* This was a dilemma Dr. D certainly needed to discuss with one of her colleagues. She thought, *I will bring the issue up at the next peer-review meeting.* Therapists meet with a clinical supervisor or in groups to discuss difficult cases and seek help from more experienced colleagues.

"Bertha, who is my next appointment? It has been a long day, and I think I may leave a little early." Dr. D didn't leave immediately; instead she stayed for a few more minutes and stared at the empty chair where her client sat earlier. She sat motionless for what seemed an eternity, wondering what to do next. Finally she mustered the strength and courage to get up and leave the office. Yes, courage. Dr. D was not ready to return to her apartment. It is difficult to be alone with one's thoughts in a tiny apartment. Each time Dr. D heard a story about a woman in pain, it opened her heart and mind to the missing piece in her own puzzle.

Dr. D finally made her way to the car. The drive seemed shorter than usual because she was preoccupied by Nicolette's story; it monopolized her thoughts and kept her from thinking about the traffic and the drive home. As she drove, she noted that everything else that day took a back seat to the very traumatic story her client narrated earlier. *How do I process Nicollet's story?* Question after question plagued her mind. She did not even notice that she was right in front of the apartment building.

"Home at last!" Her excitement was short-lived as she noticed that the elevator was out of service again. She sighed as she slowly walked up the stairs. Each step felt like a painful move toward facing the truth about her own struggles. "Made it!" She exclaimed once she reached the top of the stairs. "Hello, Casper, how is my baby today? Was your day as long and tedious as mine?" *My dog is my sounding board at the end of a long, grueling, day,* she thought to herself. "I wish John was here for me like you are, Casper. Maybe I will call him before I go to sleep. Who knows? He may have some tips for handling a situation as delicate as reporting Nicolette's abuse. Shall we watch a little television before I call John?" Dr. D never called her fiancé. She talked, Casper listened, and they both fell asleep on the couch.

Inner Beauty

The Sixth Session: Rachel's Story

"The alarm startled me! I can't believe it is 6:30 a.m. Casper, I have to get dressed quickly because I have an early appointment with Eve." Dr. D was amazed that she still felt such thrill to work with her new client after five sessions. "Are you staying in bed, sleepyhead?"

Casper looked at her and curled up in the bed as if to say, "Don't bother me." She ignored his attitude and continued chatting away. "I don't remember the last time I felt so energized going into the office. Casper, are you listening?"

Dr. D often dealt with her loneliness by talking to Casper. Sometimes it seemed like she expected a response from her dog. Dr. D continued her discourse, ignoring the fact that Casper fell asleep. "Generally at this juncture in the therapeutic relationship, my client and I would have discussed the problem a few times, often anticipating what may occur in the next session. Not so with this client. Can you believe that, Casper? Each session feels like it is the first one." Casper raised his head briefly when she took a breath. Perhaps he wished that his human mom would stop torturing him with her fancy words. Dr. D did not get the clue, she went on discussing her thoughts, stopping for brief periods. "Casper, have you seen my shoes?" The question interrupted the flow of the previous conversation about Eve. "Oh, I found them. I am late, Casper, so we will resume this conversation when I get home from work." Dr. D quickly rushed out the door and into her car. The drive to the office was filled with thoughts about the last session and how she might interact with Eve during this session.

"Good morning, Bertha, how are you doing? Is Eve here? Send her in. I am ready to see her." My client walked in the office with a new pep in her step, looking ten years younger. She wore designer jeans, a blue cashmere sweater with a scooped neck, hoop earrings with diamonds, and her signature loose bun with a few curls lightly brushing her shoulders.

"Hello, Dr. D, this will be our last session." Eve announced her impending departure without hesitation or warning.

"What?" Dr. D blurted out, not realizing that her words were audible. "Sorry, I didn't realize I said that out loud. I must admit, I was not prepared to hear this announcement, at least not this soon." Eve must have noticed the shock on her face along with her outward expression of utter surprise.

In an effort to relieve the awkward tension, Eve quickly stated, "Don't worry, Dr. D, I have another story to tell before I leave."

Dr. D's expression must have been priceless. She felt perplexed by the surge of emotions going through her. She was not worried about hearing another story; she was just not ready to let go of this client. Eve interrupted her thoughts as if she was able to read her mind. "Dr. D, would you like to hear about Rachel?" In typical Eve fashion, she pulled out her tablet and began a new story. Eve did not allow Dr. D to process the previous announcement nor ask questions.

"Nineteen-year-old Rachel found herself single and pregnant, unprepared for the journey that would lead to motherhood. Not a totally unfamiliar story, except Rachel was being groomed for greatness. From the time she could talk, she stood in front of the family and made eloquent speeches in preparation to address future followers. Rachel was unprepared, however, to give one of the most important speech of her life. Instead she opted to write a letter to her mom and dad announcing her pregnancy—words that pierced the McCarthy family's heart and shook them to the core.

"Rachel's story is one that is played out daily in families all over the world. This nineteen-year-old, however, was not your average teenager. Rachel was going to be a future spiritual leader. *What kind of leader am I?* Rachel wondered, thinking about the choice she made to sleep with a guy she hardly knew. *A leader,* Rachel thought, *is someone who can influence others. Who will listen to a single mom who did not finish college?*"

In a very unconventional way, Dr. D gasped and placed her hand on her heart which caused Eve to pause. This was an unusual response for a therapist; however, nothing about this therapeutic alliance was normal. "I am sorry, I feel bad for that young woman."

"Why?" Eve asked with a surprised look on her face.

"Well, that young woman thought her life was over." Dr. D was just as surprised by her own reaction as Eve was. She realized that she stepped out of the confines of her role as a counselor and took on a parental role.

Eve laid the tablet on her lap and looked at her therapist with some level of intensity before saying, "It is in our darkest hour that we embrace change."

"I understand. However, sometimes change comes at a steep cost," Dr. D replied.

Eve calmly picked up the tablet and continued reading the story. "I remember my mom told me that God would give me beauty for ashes. At the time, I didn't understand what she meant." It was obvious by her reaction that Dr. D was unfamiliar with the term; however, she opted to remain silent while Eve proceeded with the story. "Unfortunately when my life took a downturn and I felt as if I was going to crash and burn, I finally understood what Mom meant when she said beauty for ashes. However, at this point, the beauty part of the proverb was hard to imagine. How was beauty to emerge from the wreckage of my life? I feared that others would discover the ugliness buried beneath the beautiful exterior my parents so meticulously crafted. They could not see what I felt. I didn't fit in. It's interesting. Some of the most popular people are lonely and insecure.

"The tall slender girl with the olive skin, raven hair, and hazel eyes was not as confident as she appeared. No matter how much you tell a person that they are beautiful, they won't believe it until it resonates in their soul! My mom and dad always told me that inner beauty was much more important than the beauty people could see on the outside. They explained that one day, the exterior veil will disappear, giving access to what is found on the inside. I thought I had many years before the exterior veil of physical beauty would diminish in importance or even vanish. Like many young adults, I focused on maintaining the part of me everyone could see. The problem was while I carefully maintained the exterior self, I slowly lost track of the inner self."

Beauty for Ashes

Eve took a deep breath before proceeding with Rachel's story. "I found Rachel to be a compelling young woman. She was wise beyond her years yet very naïve." Eve spoke firmly, but her demeanor was that of a concerned parent, resigned to accepting the shenanigans of a teenager. "Rachel's story goes deeper than it appears. Life is not one-dimensional," Eve explained. "As we peel back each layer of the story, we realize that sometimes, we want what others want for us— just not at the same time. Youth has a way of interfering with wisdom."

"What do you mean?" Dr. D asked, hoping to get some clarity. It seemed as if Eve did not hear her or simply chose to ignore the therapist.

Eve attempted to proceed with the story, but Dr. D interrupted one more time. "What's wrong?" she asked, concerned that she might be overwhelmed by the details.

Dr. D saw something in her client's eyes that concerned her. Eve looked somber as if she understood Rachel's pain. Dr. D wondered if Rachel's story was in some way connected to Eve's story. "Sometimes it is easier to recount our own stories through the eyes of someone else's." Dr. D said to Eve, hoping to elicit some insight. She wondered if her goal was to elicit insight from her client or herself. She did not allow her thoughts to linger very long. Instead she tuned back in to Eve's story.

"I'm writing this letter to tell you that trauma is not always what happens to you but can result from the thoughts you allow your mind to cherish. If you think you are a failure and believe it, then you are. How tragic it could be to derail the life you are supposed to live because of a negative thought. We live in an era in which people blame the choices they make on past trauma but fail to use their authority over the thoughts that continue to retraumatize them. Many suffered and are suffering great trauma, but our trauma does not have to define who we become."

"Wow!" Dr. D exclaimed, wondering whose trauma Eve spoke of. "Are these your words or Rachel's?" she asked her client but did not get a response. Eve simply continued to read Rachel's story.

"This may not be a popular letter. Many of you may disagree with the notion that we bear some responsibility for what happens in our lives. Our journey is never an easy one, we encounter many obstacles on our path. Annoying rocks, painful boulders, debris from the wreckage of the lives of relatives and friends, murky waters from the floods of our negative thoughts, the steep incline of our insecurities all produce challenges that threaten our walk.

"My journey was temporarily sidetracked because I took my eyes off my purpose and turned a deaf ear to the inner voice that guided me. I learned that the exterior veil is more fragile than it appears. One stressful event can tear it down, exposing the vulnerable person below the surface. What dwells beneath your veil? When was the last time you took a look? Each question poured from my mind without the prospect of a response. The truth is, beneath the veil hid the most vulnerable part of me."

Eve took several deep breaths before carefully resting her tablet on the small table beside the chair. She turned her attention to the therapist and asked what she thought about the story thus far.

Dr. D reflected on her response for a few second. She looked at Eve like she was studying her client. "I don't know, Eve." Both the story and the question left Dr. D unable to formulate a cogent response. Dr. D paused while trying to search for the appropriate words. She hoped an answer would magically fall from the sky. "I guess I am waiting until you are finished so I can ask some questions about Rachel."

Frustrated by the way she responded to her client, Dr. D muttered under her breath, "You could have come up with a more creative answer." Perhaps she should have used this opportunity to delve further into Eve's story; but she didn't.

Before Dr. D could revise her response, Eve announced that she was going to proceed with the story. "Dr. D, it is quite okay if you do not have a response. I will go on reading the story. "I was too young to have a baby! What will my parents say? What would my friends think? What will become of me? Rachel wondered aloud as she fought hard to keep the tears from streaming down her face. My saving grace was the baby girl I almost kept from gracing this world. My fear of failure prompted me to try and terminate the pregnancy. Or so I thought! All I remember was walking out of the make-shift clinic, thinking about the child I could have had. I wondered about the gender of my baby. I apologized for not being able to keep her/him. Yes, I apologized for not being the mother he or she needed me to be. I said a prayer asking for forgiveness and took the medication to terminate the pregnancy. In those days, 'backstreet' doctors gave young women medicine to terminate their pregnancy. Although legal, abortion was still considered immoral.

"I took so much of the stuff, I become very ill. However, watching the blood and parts of my baby exit my body was even more gut-wrenching. 'I am sorry,' I muttered, not understanding the full implications of my action. 'I am sorry, I am sorry, I am sorry.' I repeated again and again, trying to comprehend what I had done.

"Two months after taking the stuff, I sat in the living room, feeling sorry for myself as I grieved the loss of my baby. I remembered feeling a dull but nagging pain in my stomach. My stomach was still bloated, and I assumed I was going to start my period. I decided to go to the doctor because I continued to feel unwell. The second day of March—I will never forget that day—two major events happened. My birthday was the following week, and I found out that I was still pregnant. After getting a sonogram, Dr. Douglass walked in the room, and his words hit me like a ton of bricks. 'The baby looks okay!' What! Suddenly I felt the room spin as I braced myself to keep from falling. I could hardly believe what I heard. I did not tell anyone that I was pregnant because I knew I would terminate the pregnancy. 'What do you mean the baby is okay?' I asked, hoping there was a misunderstanding. How could this be possible? I asked myself over and over. I saw what I thought was the baby exit my body.

"If I did not believe in the power of God before, this experience made me a believer. I remembered thinking, *How can this be possible?* This thought was immediately replaced by another one—this child must be special. My baby girl came in the fall, and she was perfect. When I looked into her eyes for the first time, I saw the future my fears almost ripped from me. God placed his hand inside my womb and protected her. He held her firmly in a corner of my body, out of the reach of the forces meant to wrench her from me. God gave me beauty for ashes. In the midst of the vestiges emerged the beauty of life.

"This letter is not intended to discourage you or to make you feel guilty for the choices you have made. It is meant to empower you, to help you discover the true beauty within. You must nurture the beauty that emerges from the ashes—"

I interrupted Eve, once again, when I saw a tear roll down her cheek. "What are you feeling?" I asked, being aware of my own emotions.

"I wondered about the dash in that child's life," Eve responded without looking up. "The dash in her life would have been much shorter if God did not intervene."

"Eve, is God intervening in your life right now?" I asked, not prepared for the answer.

"Is he intervening in your life, Dr. D?" Eve responded with a question.

"I am not sure how to answer that question. Remember we are here to discuss you." I was very cognizant of the religious overtones and the faint tugging in my heart each time we spoke of God's intervention in these stories.

For a few seconds, Dr. D's mind checked out. She found herself hovering above the office, looking down at her client. *What's happening?* she began to wonder about her sanity. For the first time, she disconnected from her client and focused completely on her feelings.

Very unusual for a therapist to focus on self rather than on the client. Therapists are trained to focus on the client (client-centered therapy). Most importantly, they are taught that the session is all about the client, not about the therapist (Dr. D realized that she had to put her client's feelings ahead of her own). Suddenly as if by magic, she returned to her office with a greater awareness of her surroundings. Eve did not miss a beat; she continued talking about Rachel. She did not seem to notice Dr. D's brief disconnection from the session.

The session did not go on for much longer. Eve stood up and announced that their time was up. At this juncture in the therapeutic relationship, Dr. D had become accustomed to Eve taking control of the session—when it started and when it ended. "Would you like to set up another appointment? I asked, hoping we would have a chance to talk about her issues—the issue that brought this client to my office.

Eve made a simple statement. "This is my last session with you."

She was taken back by the announcement but immediately reverted to therapist-mode. "Eve, while I appreciate that you feel empowered to make decisions about your life, I am concerned that we have to appropriately discuss what brought you to my office. In what ways would a follow-up appointment benefit you?" Dr. D asked the question but was keenly aware of the discourse going on in her mind. Dr. D had become extremely attached to Eve who seemed aware of the unhealthy connection.

"Dr. D, you asked if I would benefit from a follow-up appointment. I don't think I would benefit as much you," Eve replied with a half-smile which shocked Dr. D. She barely heard Eve's reply because she struggled to silence the alarm bells in her head. The alarms indicated that her client was not ready to disengage from therapy, neither was she. It took a while before Eve's last statement resonated with Dr. D. She was caught a little off balance but soon regained her composure.

Did my client say that a follow-up appointment with her would help me? Dr. D asked herself. Once again, Eve's keen ability to provoke an emotional response left Dr. D dumbfounded. "What did you mean by your last statement?" Dr. D asked as she grappled with Eve's announcement.

"Dr. D, when was the last time you talked to your fiancé face-to-face?" A poignant question that left the therapist speechless again. Dr. D knew better than to fall into Eve's trap. She felt her head spin but remained quiet for a second.

"I am not sure what you mean, Eve. I don't discuss my personal business with clients." Dr. D was sure Eve noticed her defensive posture but played it off.

"Maybe you should discuss your personal business with someone." Eve's statement created a role reversal that left the therapeutic alliance off-balance. The exchange also left Dr. D feeling more vulnerable than she could handle. However, she chose to proceed with the session.

The sixth and final session ended unceremoniously but left her feeling sad and unaccomplished. She failed to help her client! She still didn't know why Eve came to see her. They never really discussed her problem. Or did they? Dr. D was left confused; she felt as if she was the puzzle her client often talked about—a puzzle undone.

The drive home was long and peppered with a barrage of questions swirling in the therapist's head. *I feel helpless and hopeless, not knowing how to tap into the pain that led Eve to my office.* She wondered if she should have been more forceful. *Should I have required Eve to discuss her issues rather than spending so much time reading stories? But what if they were not mere stories? What did I miss? Will I ever see Eve again?* One question after another popped up in her head. The questions finally stopped when she pulled up in front of her apartment building.

Home sweet home! I have never felt so happy to see my little apartment. I miss my dog. Those were her first thoughts, but her elation quickly turned to sadness—she felt like she was approaching a tomb rather than her apartment. "Casper, where are you?" Her faithful friend did not greet her at the door; instead there was silence. Darkness enveloped the apartment, and Dr. D felt disoriented. "What's happening to me? Where am I?" The last thing she remembered was talking with Eve about terminating therapy. Trapped in a haze of confusion, she stumbled around the apartment, looking for her beloved dog. "The last time I saw him was this morning before leaving for work. Casper, where are you?" Dr. D said out loud, hoping someone would hear her. After a few minutes searching the apartment, she was unable to find Casper and instead began calling for her fiancé. "John, where are you?" She was suddenly overcome by loneliness; the apartment felt smaller, and the walls began to close in on her—she felt trapped. The small eclectic sanctuary all of a sudden felt like a tomb. It offered no way of escape.

The only way she could explain what was happening to her was by equating the experience to entering an alternate reality. "Everyone seemed to disappear—my dog, my fiancé, and even Eve. Where did everyone go?" She heard her voice asking the question over and over but was unable to figure out what was going on. Thinking about the earlier meeting with Eve made her confusion even more pronounced. Even the memory of working with her client seemed unreal. "Who was she?"

Someone calling her name pierced the haze that trapped Dr. D in the apartment. She felt herself transported to a place she did not recognize, sucked through a time warp of sorts. She heard a faint voice beckoning her to listen to instructions. The voice was not very forceful but commanded her attention. *I don't understand what is happening. Where did everyone go?* Dr. D asked over and over in her head as she tried to open her eyes. The darkness in her mind prevented her from seeing who was calling and where she was.

Part 3

Acceptance

"Eve, it is time for your appointment with the psychiatrist." The high-pitched sound resonating in the room was the voice of a young nurse assigned to the hospital ward. Eve's eyes remained closed as she fought to open them. "Why is she not responding?"

"Eve, can you hear me?" Frustrated, the nurse turned to the senior psychiatric technician who knew Eve best. "Why doesn't she respond?"

"Call her Dr. D," Angel said as he offered a reassuring wink. "She told the admitting nurse that her name was Dr. Mary E. Di Angelo."

"Dr. D, can you hear me? I am Maria, the ward nurse?" Eve finally opened her eyes but was confused and did not know where she was. "Hi, Eve, welcome to the land of the living. I will be right back," Maria said jokingly before stepping outside the room to talk with Angel.

Maria cornered Angel in the hallway to inquire about their new patient. "What's her story?" The nurse asked, trying to gather information about Eve.

Angel did not respond. Instead he reminded Maria to be gentle with the patient. "She needs our patience and compassion."

"Okay," Maria agreed, not completely understanding Angel's rationale for making the statement. The nurse and technician glanced at each other but did not say another word before going back into Eve's room.

"Hello, Eve, how are you feeling?" Angel, the psychiatric technician, asked. Eve did not respond. Instead she looked around the room before her eyes landed on the nurse who was standing in the doorway. Noting Eve's discomfort with her new environment, Angel sought to put her at ease. "Maria is one of our most loving and capable nurses. She will take good care of you." Angel said in an effort to comfort the new patient. Angel was the strong silent type, a man of few words; he simply started cleaning up the medication tray before exiting the room. His exit from the room and Maria's entry almost seemed choreographed, like the changing of the guards.

"Hello, my name is Maria, and I am going to take over your care, but Angel will still be available to help." Maria reassured Eve.

"Well, Eve, I mean Dr. D, it is just the two of us now. How about I help you get dressed and walk you to Dr. Lord's office?" Dr. Lord's office was located on the seventh floor of the hospital. He was the senior psychiatrist. In fact, he was the most senior doctor in the hospital.

"Easy does it!" Maria the nurse exclaimed. "I know psychiatric medication can make you a bit dizzy, but they are meant to help you. Here we go, Dr. D, just step into the elevator, and we will be on our way." The ride up to Dr. Lord's office was slow and for the most part, punctuated by silence. Maria tried her best to engage Eve in conversation to no avail. "Dr. D, do you have children?" She did not wait for a response from Eve, instead Maria continued talking a mile a minute. "I have two girls, ten and eight. Leslie is my ten-year-old. She is vivacious and full of life. Joanna is the eight-year-old. She is shy but loves to help. They are doing so well in school. I am proud of them. I have been married for eleven years, how about you?" Eve hardly took her gaze off the floor, but it did not deter Maria from talking. In fact, Maria did not wait for a response from Eve; she continued talking until they reached the seventh floor.

The elevator finally came to a stop, and the doors slowly opened to reveal an expansive waiting room. Maria said loudly, "Eve, look at the beautiful gold carpet." The nurse gushed as they both stepped out of the elevator onto the most opulent gold carpet. The eggshell-colored walls shimmered as if they were encrusted with millions of crushed diamonds. Jewel-encrusted chandeliers hung in the vestibule. The jewels sparkled and reflected light from the walls, diminishing the need for artificial light. *How odd*, Maria thought. She had never been up to the seventh floor before. The seventh floor looked vastly different from the rest of the hospital. Without hesitating, the women proceeded to the semicircular desk located in the center of the room.

"Hello, I am Nurse Maria Davis. I brought Eve for her appointment with Dr. Lord."

"Hello, Eve, Dr. Lord will be right with you," the receptionist greeted them with a warm smile as she directed Eve to the waiting room.

A booming male voice that echoed throughout the waiting room caught the women's attention. "Hello, Eve!" Eve looked up and for the first time, there was a twinkle in her eyes. She responded to the greeting with a low-toned hello to Dr. Lord. *Finally a sign of life in Eve's dull eyes*, Maria thought to herself but did not dare say it out loud. "How are you?" Dr. Lord asked, using a rhetorical tone that gave the impression he already knew the answer.

"I'm not sure." Eve's response seemed dull. Her monotone voice was a clear indication that she was sad.

Maria asked Dr. Lord to talk in private. "Sure, come on back to my office," Dr. Lord graciously responded. Maria was eager to give Dr. Lord the run down on his new patient. "Eve is new on the ward and tends to isolate herself, keeping other patients at arm's length. She doesn't talk and has had no visitors since being hospitalized. Her real name is Eve M. Di Angelo or Maria E. Di Angelo. We are not too sure. She has been hospitalized for two days now, following the tragic death of her husband (at least that is what she reported, but we have not been able to corroborate her story)." Maria talked a mile a minute. She hardly took a breath. "There are no known relatives, and I don't think she has any children. A neighbor called 911 when they heard screaming and a big thud, or maybe they saw smoke and called 911. I am not sure. The details are sketchy, but it seems Eve had some type of break with reality and began banging on the walls and screaming before falling to the floor."

Dr. Lord stood in amazement at the number of words per minute Maria was able to produce. Still unaware that Dr. Lord wanted to say something, Maria continued talking. "The woman who came with her to the ER said she was a neighbor who attended the same church. She also said that there was a fire in the apartment, and Eve's parents died in the fire. We don't have all the details, but I know that there is an ongoing police investigation."

Maria did jabber on even though she was unsure of the details. Dr. Lord interrupted for a brief second. "There is a lot to unpack." Maria shook her head and went on.

"Angel, the psychiatric technician, told me that she likes to be called Dr. D." Maria barely emerged for air. She continued talking about the details surrounding Eve's hospitalization without taking a breath. "I really think that Eve might be hiding something." Maria's last statement was the final straw.

Dr. Lord interrupted Maria's ramblings with the following statement, "I need to see my client now. I wonder if Eve would be comfortable giving me the details I need to help her?" Dr. Lord's fatherly tone was stern but caring. Maria quickly got the clue. She immediately stopped talking and walked out the office. Eve was waiting nearby in the waiting room. "Hello, Eve, are you ready to get started?" Dr. Lord asked. She remained silent but did acknowledge Dr. Lord with a nod while she continued to gaze at the floor.

"Eve, did you hear what Dr. Lord said?" Maria asked, but Dr. Lord intervened.

"That's okay, Eve and I will talk later in my office." Eve never said a word but picked up her head and looked at Dr. Lord.

Once again, Maria tried to engage Eve by referring to her as Dr. D. "This is Dr. Lord, your new psychiatrist. He will take good care of you." Maria tried her best to reassure Eve that everything would be fine, to no avail.

Sensing that Maria needed some help and Eve needed a break from the nonstop chatter, Dr. Lord gently took charge of the conversation by restating his greeting. "Hello, Eve, that is your name, isn't it?" Dr. Lord asked in a very soothing tone. His voice elicited a visible sigh of relief from Eve.

His baritone voice echoed like a trumpet, but it brought a sense of tranquility that made Eve feel secure. "Yes, that is my name!" For the first time in two days, Eve responded verbally and provided uninterrupted eye contact. It was as if she intuitively knew Dr. Lord will care for her. It seemed as if she recognized his voice from some past encounter.

"I will pick you up in an hour," Maria said as she went toward the elevator.

Eve nodded and entered the office. "Have a seat, Eve," Dr. Lord said as he motioned to the wingback chair. Almost immediately following the exchange between Eve and Dr. Lord, there was a knock on the door which was left ajar.

Hope, the nurse from the seventh floor, peeked into Dr. Lord's office to see if he was already with the new patient she saw in the emergency room. "Hi, Dr. Lord, I just wanted to see if you had a chance to talk to the new patient." Generally nurses and technicians do not interrupt the therapy session unless there is an emergency. However, since the door was not completely closed, Hope figured she might peek inside. "Hi, Eve, remember me? It's Hope. I'm the psychiatric nurse that greeted you when you were first hospitalized."

Hope was the charge nurse on the seventh floor but worked the evening shift in the ER the day Eve was admitted. Occasionally Hope was assigned to the ER to care for patients who were not expected to recover. She was a great listener and comforter. Many of her patients seemed to make a miraculous comeback, earning her the nickname "the miracle worker."

Hope's post on the seventh floor gave her a unique perspective of psychiatric patients admitted to the ER. From her vantage point, Nurse Hope saw devastation caused by patients' feelings of helplessness and hopelessness. She helped with the care of the most fragile individuals—those whose lives seem meaningless but found hope in knowing someone cared for their suffering.

Nurse Hope was a small-framed woman with very nondescript features—she had a kind face and beautiful demeanor. Her thousand-watt smile energized and calmed patients who otherwise saw no point in living. Nurse Hope's calm demeanor was flanked by a commanding presence that told patients they had nothing to worry about. Her favorite catch phrase, "I got you," became a safety net for individuals who felt as if they were falling from a precipice.

Once patients realized that she was there to help them, they loved and clung to her. She prayed that Eve would open up and trust her desire to help, but she realized that very depressed patients need a lifesaver to keep them from going over the Niagara Falls-like precipice of depression. Eve, for example, seemed adrift and heading toward deep dark waters. Without Hope, she might be drawn by the strong currents of depression and pulled under water. The psychiatric nurse was very familiar with the sentiment most depressed patients described as swimming in dark waters. Her clients often described depression as a watery-grave.

Hope addressed Eve for a second time. "Do you remember me?"

Finally Eve responded, "Yes, I remember you." Her monotone voice reflected her sadness and struggle to express her feelings. She did not even lift her head to acknowledge Hope's presence; in fact, it was as if she carried the weight of the world on her shoulders. Although Eve did not give eye contact to the psychiatric nurse, there was some connection between the two women. Their relationship was hard to explain. They only met a few days before, but Eve seemed vaguely familiar with Hope. The push-pull between feelings of familiarity and rejection of Hope could only be described as Eve's desire to live as she dealt with fear of the unknown. Hope continued to engage Eve and Dr. Lord in small talk.

In the meantime, Maria doubled back to remind Dr. Lord to send a copy of his note to the fourth floor. She walked up and interrupted the exchange between Hope and Eve. "Sorry, Dr. Lord, I forgot to tell you something." Seeing Hope and Dr. Lord in the office with Eve gave Maria a strange sense of peace. "Well, it looks like you are in good hands with Hope and Dr. Lord. Please have Hope or one of the nurses contact me when you are finished with your appointment. I am going back to the fourth-floor ward but will pick you up when you are finished meeting with Dr. Lord." Maria almost forgot the reason she went back to Dr. Lord's office. Although, somehow, Maria knew Eve would be well-cared for. She also felt that Eve was comfortable with her surroundings because of her calmer demeanor.

As she walked toward the elevator, Maria reminded herself to pick up her patient in an about an hour. Eve had a powerful effect on the people she met—Maria was no different. As she got on the elevator, she thought to herself, *Eve reminds me of an enigma, perhaps a puzzle that is hard to piece together. It was difficult to estimate her age, race, or ethnicity. Most importantly, trying to decipher Eve was challenging.*

Eve was a small-framed, very fit woman in her thirties or forties with the body of a thirty-year-old woman. No one knew for sure how old she was because she had no documentation with her. It was as if she fell from the sky or just appeared. She had curly blond hair—so tightly curled, it looked like she was wearing an afro wig. Her olive skin was the perfect backdrop for slanted, hazel-colored eyes. As beautiful as she was, her eyes were covered by a haze of sadness that overshadowed her beauty. The haze appeared to extinguish an inner desire for life. Her full lips did not speak a word of the secrets locked in her mind, but her eyes revealed the inner turmoil.

"Two days had passed since our first meeting, but I still remember the vacant look in her eyes—a look so empty, it made her seem like a body devoid of a soul. Sadness clouded her countenance and hid any sign she may have been a vivacious person at some point in her life. I wondered if Eve could have been someone whose life was filled with joy, family, and friends." The conversation in Maria's head became audible. Thank goodness she was alone in the elevator as she carried on the monologue.

Eve's complex features were reminiscent of an eclectic painting. The artist took the most beautiful facial features from a variety of women and skillfully wove them like a tapestry into one person. She was like a canvas sprinkled with colors from the rainbow and contained by lines and symmetry. Her maker used different ethnic and racial features to create her. She appeared as someone who could relate to anyone in the universe. Beautiful dark-olive skin, beautiful slanted eyes, tightly curled blond hair, full lips were characteristics found in so many different people. Eve was indeed a canvas upon which God poured out his masterpiece. He did not spare his power of creations. He used hues, lines, and shades borrowed from every race and cultural background to create Eve. She encompassed the best and the worst of every woman. After all, her name was given to the very first woman in the world. Eve's essence spoke to her uniqueness and God's protection of her in the book of Psalms, "For you did form my inward parts. You did cover me in my mother's womb. I will give thanks unto thee; for I am fearfully and wonderfully made" (Psalms 139:13).

Although Eve seemed to engender every woman, she often appeared disconnected from other patients and staff on the ward. During her stay, she seldom allowed others to get a glimpse inside of her world—a place most likely filled by loneliness and depression. Her wall-like sadness kept her from communicating with others and kept others from entering her world. Eve's disconnection from the world must be related to a traumatic event, the staff reasoned. However, no one dared diagnose her; they simply knew she needed help.

"Eve, can I ask you to step out for a little bit?" Hope needed a few minutes with Dr. Lord to give him a brief synopsis on his new patient. *I can only imagine who this patient really is*, Hope thought to herself before beginning her briefing with Dr. Lord. Eve did not speak to Hope prior to her meeting with Dr. Lord which occurred a couple days after being hospitalized. "How can this woman, who appeared to have so much in common with so many people on the surface, be so different?" Hope asked Dr. Lord a rhetorical question which also resonated with other hospital staff. "No one seems to know much about her except what she revealed at intake. She was confused and very sad when first responders brought her to the hospital."

Hope recalled her first meeting with Eve as she continued to brief Dr. Lord about his new patient. "I remember being on the ward the first day Eve was admitted. I saw a frail, disheveled, grief-stricken woman being escorted down the narrow hallway to one of the rooms on the fourth floor. She stared at the ground as if she was afraid the ground would disappear under her feet. This was probably a fair assumption, given she just lost her husband (at least that is what she reported upon admission). Eve's body was covered by a baggy blouse and a long dark skirt that gave the impression she had no legs." Hope paused for a second and gazed at the ceiling as if trying to remember more details. “I can still see the vision of her long skirt floating down the hallway in a ghost-like manner—how appropriate for someone who lost their footing in life? She carried an overnight bag over her shoulder and clasped a notebook in her right hand, so tightly the blood seemed to disappear from her fingers. I reasoned that her notebook contained top secret information she wanted to guard with her life.

“I managed to get a glimpse at the notebook before securing it in the locker. I saw page after page of stories documenting the lives of women Eve claimed were her clients. The pages in her notebook unfolded adversity and triumph in the lives of the women she wrote about. The writing on those pages left me wondering if the stories inadvertently revealed a glimpse into Eve’s life—”

“Hope, I am ready to see Eve.” Dr. Lord abruptly interrupted Hope’s account of his patient to remind her that he was ready to start the session.

“Oh, sorry, Dr. Lord.” Hope walked out to the lobby where Eve sat, waiting to be called into the office. “Eve, I will see you later.” The nurse said to the patient, expecting some form of acknowledgement that never came.

First Session with Dr. Lord

“Hello, Eve,” Dr. Lord greeted his new patient with a smile.

“Hello, Dr. Lord,” Eve responded as she slowly walked into the office and took a seat on a blue love seat facing the door.

“I am sorry for all the interruptions. How are you feeling today? Hope told me a little bit about you, and I read the intake paperwork. Why do you think you are here?” Dr. Lord leaned forward in his chair and looked at Eve with compassion.

“I don’t remember,” Eve responded as she glanced at the floor. “I think I lost someone important, but I cannot remember who.”

“Let me help you,” Dr. Lord said in a soft tone. “The information in your file says that you reported losing your husband recently.

Is that true?" Eve did not acknowledge being married nor did she directly respond to Dr. Lord's statement.

She sighed after a long pause before speaking. "I miss John." She did not reveal if John was her husband or someone else.

"Would you like to talk about John?" Dr. Lord suggested that talking might help her recover her memories.

"I am not ready to talk about him."

"That's all right, Eve, you don't have to talk about anything you are not ready to discuss. Since you don't want to talk about John, what would you like to talk about?"

Eve did not answer the question but instead asked a question of her own. "Would you like to hear a story?"

Curious, Dr. Lord agreed. "I would like to hear your story!" he exclaimed. Eve must have been caught off guard by his response. She leaned back in her seat with a surprised look on her face but did not verbally convey her feelings.

Following a few awkward seconds, Eve said, "I feel lost."

Dr. Lord looked at his patient again with compassion. "Why?"

Eve did not know how to respond to the question. She gathered her thoughts and tried to explain. "I feel as if…" Her voice trailed.

"How do you feel?" Dr. Lord prompted his patient.

"I feel as if I'm disappearing. Nothing feels real at this moment. You know; like a watermark on a page."

"It must be difficult to feel like no one sees you. Have you ever felt that way before? Let me rephrase, have you ever not felt real?" Dr. Lord was cognizant that his question could potentially backfire.

"Yes, I think I had a life, family, and friends."

Dr. Lord looked at Eve intently and leaned in toward her once again. "What happened to the people in your life?" Following another awkward pause, Eve leaned back in the chair for what seemed to be an eternity. The patient allowed her tears to quietly flow down her cheek and shrugged her shoulders, indicating that she did not have a response to Dr. Lord's question.

Most of the session was punctuated by silence. Dr. Lord did not want to push his visibly-fragile patient, fearing she would decompensate (a psychological term that simply means she might crack under pressure). Instead he opted to back off and ask less intrusive questions. "Eve, would you indulge me by telling me what comes to mind when I mention the following words?" Eve looked perplexed but agreed to go along with Dr. Lord's request.

DR. LORD. Ship
EVE. Voyage
DR. LORD. Where
EVE. Adrift
DR. LORD. Sea
EVE. Turbulence
DR. LORD. Sail
EVE. Freedom
DR. LORD. Family
EVE. Pause

Following the short pause, Eve stood up and said she was ready to go back to her room. "Are you okay?" Dr. Lord asked, concerned because of Eve's sudden reaction.

"You said I did not have to talk about topics that made me uncomfortable." Dr. Lord was a little confused by Eve's response to the exercise since she agreed to it.

However, Dr. Lord reluctantly complied with their agreement. Although he did not completely let her off the hook. "If we changed the subject, would you continue talking?"

"No, I am a little tired and would like Maria to come and get me." Okay. Dr. Lord reassured Eve that she would not be pressed to talk about difficult subjects right now. However, she would eventually have to deal with the trauma that brought her to the hospital's emergency room.

Back on the Ward

"Esperanza, please call the fourth floor and let the staff know that Eve is ready to go back to her room."

"Sure, Dr. Lord. I will call Maria to come and escort Eve back to her room." It was not long before Maria appeared in the waiting room on the seventh floor.

"Hello, Eve," Maria greeted the patient with a welcoming smile that visibly brought relief to her exasperated patient. "How was your session? Are you ready to go back to your room?"

"Sure," Eve responded in a low, monotone voice. The elevator ride and the walk down the hallway were again punctuated by silence. "Did you like Dr. Lord?" Maria interrupted the silence in an attempt to engage Eve, to no avail. The remainder of their trek back to the room seemed longer than the journey to the seventh floor.

It had been four days since Eve was first escorted down that long hallway. This time, she wore a hospital gown, and her notebook was secured in a locker. Eve shuffled as she walked to her room, lifting her head occasionally to look at the staff. She still had that vacant, expressionless look in her eyes, covered by tightly curled tresses that hung in front of her face. Eve seemed disconnected from everyone around her especially from other patients. Staff described her as a beautiful empty shell. Only an intermittent glimmer of light (like a flashlight that was turned on and off) served as a reminder of the person who once occupied the now-empty shell.

Beside the occasional outburst about her private practice, Eve remained inconspicuous. Once in a while and without warning, she would yell, "I need to get to my office." Unaware she was a patient in a hospital, she interacted with nurses and technicians as if they were her staff. "Who is my next patient?" "Where is Bertha, my secretary?" On one occasion, Eve became visibly agitated when the staff on the ward were unable to answer her questions. "Eve, honey, it is time for your p.m. medication." The night-shift nurse said gently. "We will tell Bertha that you are looking for her after you have taken your medication." The staff was always able to calm Eve and guide her to her room without much resistance.

"Whew! What a shift," the night nurse exclaimed as she briefed Maria on the events of the previous night. "I am exhausted."

"Why?" Maria asked before she started dispensing the a.m. medications to her patients.

"We will talk later. I have to finish my notes," the night-shift nurse responded as she hurried off.

"Good morning, Eve, how are you?" Maria asked as she took her patients' vital signs and helped them with their medication. "Are you ready to see Dr. Lord?"

"Yes!" Eve responded in an unusually upbeat tone. She looked at Maria with hope in her eyes. The look spoke of a renewed commitment to get back into the game of life. Unfortunately the look in Eve's eyes and her demeanor were short-lived. She reverted to her signature downcast look as the pair started their journey back to the seventh floor.

Eve and Maria walked slowly toward the elevator while Eve stared at the floor, and Maria continued being her usual chatty self. Eve simply nodded or responded with monosyllables to Maria's questions but never really engaged in the conversation. "Are you listening?" the nurse occasionally stopped talking to ensure her patient was still with her but did not force her to talk. Maria always took her cues from Eve and allowed her to walk in silence, perhaps contemplating her visit with Dr. Lord. "Eve, we are here." Maria's voice seemed to wake Eve from a trance.

"Oh, okay!" Eve's responses seldom disclosed her inner turmoil, but it is hard to keep a lid on boiling water. Even when we don't intentionally reveal ourselves, our silence exposes our inner struggle and gives the world a glimpse of who we are.

Second Session with Dr. Lord

"Good morning, Dr. Lord, I brought Eve for her appointment," Maria greeted the psychiatrist before heading toward the elevator. Dr. Lord greeted his patient as he motioned to Maria to wait.

"Eve, do you mind if I talk with Maria before we meet?" Eve nodded and took a seat in the waiting room. Come on in, Maria. Please have a seat."

Before Dr. Lord could say a word, Maria blurted out, "Is Eve a multiple?" Realizing that she spoke out loud and how it may have sounded to Dr. Lord, she reframed the question. "Do you think Eve has multiple personality disorder?" Maria was fairly new to the mental-health field and still unsure about hospital protocols and patient confidentiality.

"What do you mean?" Dr. Lord asked, realizing that Maria meant no harm. She simply wanted to understand Eve. "Occasionally we wish we could get into another person's head, but it is not an easy feat. Trying to understand what they are experiencing sometimes seem impossible." He did not give Maria a chance to respond before asking a follow-up question. "Have you heard the saying as a man thinks, so he becomes?"

"Yes," Maria responded, not quite sure where the question would lead.

In an apparent departure from the doctor-patient-confidentiality rules, Dr. Lord began talking about his patient to the nurse. "Eve's thoughts about herself have framed her reality. In other words, what she thought about herself influenced who she became during a very traumatic time." Without any further discussion, he ended the conversation with the nurse, walked out of his office, and asked his patient to come in. Maria hurried out of Dr. Lord's office to accommodate his waiting patient.

"Hello, Eve, how are you feeling today?" He looked at her with kindness and compassion like a father looks at his child. "You are safe!" Dr. Lord spoke three words that brought unspeakable calm to Eve. It was very apparent that his patient lowered the wall she had erected—her smile and posture spoke volumes about her confidence in the upcoming session.

Eve walked in the office and sat on her favorite chair. "Hello, Dr. Lord, how are you?"

"I am well, thank you for asking." Without hesitation Dr. Lord dove into the session. "Eve, tell me a little about yourself."

"There isn't much to tell," she responded. "Why am I here?" she asked, looking a little puzzled.

"You were brought to the hospital following what can be described as a psychiatric breakdown."

"I don't remember that day," Eve said while gazing up as if trying to recall the events that brought her to the hospital. "I do recall feeling pain I never felt before. A tsunami of feelings overtook me with a force I could not endure." Eve briefly paused before stating. "I feel like you are my only help. I am not sure how to put it in words. You are my salvation—a wall that keeps the rising tide from overtaking me."

Dr. Lord seemed impressed by his patient's knack for selecting the right words to paint a picture that clearly described her feeling. "You have a compelling way with words. I wonder, however, how do we move your words from a static place to action? In other words, how do you capitalize on your faith in me to move to a place of healing?"

Dr. Lord's patient thought about the question for a second and replied, "I trust you will get me to a place of healing."

"What would your husband say?" Dr. Lord asked a very strange question, perhaps to get Eve to talk about the husband she mentioned at intake.

"What do you mean?" Eve asked, taken aback by the question. "I don't know what he would say, but I think he would be proud that I am working on myself."

Eve's connection to Dr. Lord was evident in the openness and ease with which she discussed her feelings. This was clearly new territory for Eve. She never before discussed her fears with another human being. She thought to herself that Dr. Lord had a way to put people at ease. "I feel safe and secure talking to you," Eve confided in her doctor before she continued revealing her feelings of sadness and anxiety. She also shared her feelings of loneliness and insecurity. Dr. Lord's skillful precision with words unlocked memories and feelings that were previously out of reach.

It seemed the session was going smoothly, and Eve was reaching a milestone in therapy when suddenly—she hit a landmine (an explosive device often placed right below the surface. These are triggered by the weight of a person or vehicle). Dr. Lord asked about John, a question that triggered painful memories that were too agonizing to face. Two steps forward, three steps backward.

The thought of talking about her husband caused Eve to instantaneously summon new defenses. Almost as fast as she tore the last invisible wall down, another one was erected. In an attempt to circumvent the questions, she retreated behind a wall of silence but again had a change of heart and decided to yield to Dr. Lord's guidance. The ping-pong-like change of heart surprised both Dr. Lord and Eve. She looked confused and questioned why she felt a sudden urge to relent and allow Dr. Lord to guide her through this painful and scary labyrinth.

Dr. Lord repeated his statement. "Tell me about your husband."

Instead of answering the question, Eve talked about her journey to the ER. "I don't remember coming here. In fact, I don't remember much."

"Those memories must be extremely painful."

"Yes," Eve responded, relaxing into the chair. Dr. Lord noted some hesitance in her response.

"Looks like you are having a hard time with the question," Dr. D said to his patient. Eve stated that she did not remember why she was in the hospital but answered positively to the statement about painful memories. "What are you afraid to remember?" Dr. Lord asked, hoping to further the therapeutic gain.

"I don't know. Maybe I am afraid to…" Eve's voice trailed off, followed by a long pause.

"I see that this is difficult for you, Eve."

"Yes, it is."

"Let's start with something less intimidating. Tell me about the good times with your husband."

"My husband was a fun-loving person who treated me with kindness and respect. He believed in me and supported my decision to become a therapist. I often used him as a sounding board when I had a hard day at the office. John was my constant companion like my dog, Casper. My John was easy to talk to and always put me first." Without giving a clue that something maybe wrong, Eve stopped talking and stared at the door.

"The medical staff said you were brought here because you tried to hurt yourself several times after your husband's death. Do you remember that?" Dr. Lord knew that the information was erroneous but wanted to get the correct information directly from his patient. Eve lowered her head and nodded yes. Dr. Lord continued. "A member of your church brought you to the emergency room because you had not eaten in a week. She said you tried several times to kill yourself. Is this information correct? I have been given different accounts by different staff. I am not sure which to believe. Will you help me understand this mystery?" Again she lowered her gaze but remained silent. Dr. Lord continued trying to gently elicit a response from her, to no avail.

Finally Dr. Lord stated, "I am a little confused. Church members said they were unable to find any pictures of John in the apartment. In fact, your church sisters did not know you were married. Noting Eve's discomfort with the conversation, he backed off the current line of questions. Dr. Lord's attempts to solve the mystery of John, Eve's attempted suicides, and reports that there was a fire in the apartment which killed her parents was unfruitful.

After a short period of silence, Dr. Lord decided to take a different approach. Instead of talking about the obvious disconnection in Eve's story, he decided to focus on the large diary she brought with her to the hospital. "Eve, do you remember the diary you brought with you the day you were hospitalized? Tell me about it."

Suddenly Eve asked forcefully, "What diary?"

"Actually it is a collection of stories you wrote," Dr. Lord responded. His intention was to push Eve as far as he could without pushing her over the edge. "Do you remember writing them, Eve?"

Her gaze lowered to the floor and responded in a soft tone, "Those are my client's clinical notes." For a brief moment she appeared defeated as she stared at the ground, searching for her next word.

Without a hint of hesitation or prompting from Dr. Lord, she looked at him and said, "I remember."

"What do you remember?"

To Dr. Lord's amazement, Eve took the conversation in a different direction. "I really miss John. We were married for a long time." Eve stopped momentarily but resumed talking. "I can't believe he is gone. We were happy and in love."

"How did you meet John?" Dr. Lord asked, confused by the discrepancies in her story.

"I met John in 1965 in Louisiana." There were obvious holes in her story since Eve was a child in 1965. The fact that Eve was not old enough to be married in the 1960s did not stop her from telling the story. "He was my knight in shining armor." Her story sounded similar to one of the stories in the diary she guarded so fiercely.

Dr. Lord was happy that his patient was talking and did not want to stop the process, so he waited before making the following statement. "Your story is similar to the beginning of Wanda's story. Tell me, Eve, in what ways do you relate to Wanda?"

Eve abruptly stood up and yelled, "Bertha, where are you? Is the next patient here? I need my notebook. I cannot write my clinical notes without it." Eve's sudden regression was an indication that she was not ready to deal with the repressed feelings that continued to haunt her.

Sensing that his patient was spiraling out of control, he redirected the session and tried to ground her. "Eve, let's practice our grounding exercises. I want you to run your fingers slowly across the arm of your chair. Take a deep breath and describe the fabric?"

"It feels soft and warm! It reminds me of my John—"

"How so?" Dr. Lord interrupted.

"His touches were warm and fuzzy despite his manly hands. He was always so gentle with me. I felt secure in his arms, never worried about my needs." She took a deep breath and stopped talking. The frown on her face was a clear indication of stress. Eve's physical appearance spoke volumes to the inner turmoil. Dr. Lord did not interrupt the silence; instead he allowed his patient to be in the moment rather than rush the process.

After a brief pause, Eve picked back up where she left off. She described her relationship with John in great detail. "John was kind and loving. He was also a good provider and a good husband."

"Was he a good father?" Dr. Lord asked.

Eve was obviously surprised by the question because she redirected the course of the session. She stopped talking and asked Dr. Lord, "Are you married?"

The seasoned doctor never seemed surprised by his patient's sudden outburst or questions. "No, I am not married. However, some people refer to me as a husband figure while others see me as a father figure." It was evident Dr. Lord did not want to lose momentum. He immediately guided Eve back to the conversation by asking her to elaborate more about her relationship with John.

"He was tall, blond, and handsome. He was a very kind man."

"Sounds like someone very special," Dr. Lord remarked.

"He was special to me." Sadness came over Eve's countenance as she recounted her life with John, but she did not seem as affected as she did earlier when she first introduced the topic. It was not lost on Dr. Lord the way Eve avoided the question regarding John as a father.

"I think we have made great strides today. Would you like me to call Maria to take you back to the ward?" Dr. Lord's voice interrupted Eve's thoughts.

"Yes," she responded eagerly. It was obvious the session had taken an emotional toll. "I think I am ready to go back to my room."

It was interesting to watch Dr. Lord's interaction with his patient. Although Eve was on a ward with twenty other patients, Dr. Lord treated her as if she was the only one. "I will see you tomorrow at 10:00 a.m. right after you have had your breakfast. How does that sound?"

Eve looked at Dr. Lord directly in his eyes with a big smile. "Yes, I look forward to our appointment."

Angel, one of Eve's favorite psych techs from the fourth floor, came to retrieve her. Surprisingly Eve was not initially receptive to Angel's presence in Dr. Lord's office. "Where is Maria?" Eve asked with a bit of panic in her voice.

"Maria is off for the evening," Angel reassured her. "Don't worry, Eve, I will take good care of you." Angel, who was very familiar with Eve, was an expert at calming her anxiety.

"Tell me, how was your appointment?" Angel greeted Eve with a friendly and sincere tone. Angel was one of the first persons to interact with Eve after she was admitted to the hospital.

"Oh, hello, Angel." Eve said as if she saw him for the first time standing in the doorway of Dr. Lord's office. For some reason she didn't immediately recognize him. "How are you?" Eve asked.

The psych tech was pleased to see Eve doing so well. He cordially responded to Eve's greeting "I am doing well. How are you doing?"

"I am doing well because I just met with Dr. Lord," Eve responded.

"I am glad your appointment with Dr. Lord went well. Do you think he can help you with your sadness?"

Eve gazed directly at the wall behind Angel, searching for the answer. "I don't know if anyone can take away the deep pain I feel. However, if anyone can help, I believe Dr. Lord can."

"I am glad you have a positive outlook about your sessions with Dr. Lord. Being positive always helps the healing process."

"I agree," Eve responded as they walked toward the elevator.

Unlike her long, silent walk and elevator rides with Maria, Eve did all the talking while her escort listened. Angel was the strong, silent type. Unlike Maria, he spoke mostly when spoken to. "Angel, do you have children?"

"No, ma'am, I don't have children. I heard children are a gift from God. I would have loved to have children but never had the chance to procreate." His response was the longest interaction with Eve.

Following his response, Angel allowed the patient to talk uninterrupted. "You know that Maria has a couple of kids. I believe they are girls."

It appeared that Angel was no longer listening to Eve but simply allowed her to ramble while he smiled and nodded. The walk down the hall and elevator ride to the fourth floor was swift. "Eve, we are here, honey. Are you tired?"

"No, I am not tired. In fact, I feel like talking."

Although Angel loved listening to Eve, he realized that she needed her rest. "It's getting late, and you have a long day tomorrow." Angel suggested the client should turn in early.

Like a giddy school girl, Eve skipped along as Angel escorted her to the room. The pair said goodnight by giving each other a high five before Angel went back to his station. Eve walked directly to her room, pulled out a writing pad, and immediately started scribbling some notes. She hummed softly as she feverishly wrote, ignoring the other patient in her room or the fact that the night nurse stood in the doorway asking a question. "Eve, do you need anything before my shift is over?"

Startled, Eve responded, "I am okay." She sounded strong and vibrant—almost happy! Without skipping a beat, she returned her gaze to the writing pad.

"Well, goodnight. Remember, lights out in thirty minutes," The nurse said as she turned to walk away.

"Yes, I know," Eve responded without lifting her head. Eve continued writing until she fell asleep with her pen in her hand and the writing pad next to her.

A Dream State

"Eve, are you tired?" Dr. Lord's voice floated into the room as if riding on some type of otherworldly wave. His thunder-like voice was booming and deep yet silky and pleasant.

Awakened from a deep sleep, it took a minute for Eve to realize what she was hearing. "Dr. Lord, is that you?" she asked, trying to orient herself.

"Yes, Eve, you called me."

"I don't remember calling you. The last thing I remember before falling asleep was asking God why me?"

"What was his response?"

"I didn't hear a response. Instead I heard your voice calling me." Eve was perplexed, not understanding what was happening. She looked around the room and rubbed her eyes. "Am I hearing things now?" Eve asked herself, trying to wake up. Her roommate was still asleep and did not appear to have heard Dr. Lord's voice. Eve thought for sure she was hallucinating.

Perceiving that Eve was having a hard time coming to terms with what was happening, he spoke up, "People often ask why me when they are unable to explain negative events in their lives." Dr. Lord looked at

Eve with a facial expression that was hard to decipher. Eve must not have noticed because it did not deter her.

She whispered her next question as if afraid to disclose a dark secret. "Dr. Lord, why do you think bad things happen to good people?" Eve's eyes expressed the sadness and disappointment that innocent people seem to suffer as much as bad people.

Dr. Lord pondered the question for a second before responding. "It rains on the just and the unjust, Eve. Both get wet when they leave the safety of the shelter."

"What do you mean, Dr. Lord? I don't see how your response relates to my question," Eve said, her voice shaky.

Dr. Lord tried to answer the question by relating his statement to something Eve was familiar with. "Have you ever gone out during a storm and didn't have your umbrella?"

"Yes," Eve cautiously responded, afraid that she may fall into some type of trap.

"Well, you will get wet just as a criminal running from the law during a rainstorm. Both are subject to the rain."

"I think I understand. We are all subject to seen and unseen forces in the world. I wish the innocent were protected."

Dr. Lord smiled. "Yes, I think you got it."

Dr. Lord did not waste any time. He redirected the conversation in an effort to explore core issues Eve purposefully ignored. "Tell me, Eve, what are some of John's best attributes?"

Caught off guard, Eve stuttered. "You…you…mean my husband?" She seemed a little confused by the question.

"Yes, your husband," Dr. Lord responded.

"Well, I like that he was always there for me no matter what kind of day I had. I like that I didn't have to pretend to be someone else. As a matter of fact, he never asked me to change my hairstyle, my clothing, the way I spoke, or who I was."

"Sounds like the perfect mate!" Dr. Lord paused to allow his client to process her feelings about the exchange and formulate a response, but Eve seemed unable or unwilling to respond to his comment.

After what seemed like a very long pause, Dr. Lord asked another question in an effort to keep the momentum. "Do you like who you are?"

"What do you mean? Of course I like who I am. In fact, I helped my clients to like who they were. Why do you keep calling me Eve?" Her response signaled trouble. Perhaps the pain of dealing with underlying trauma elicited by Dr. Lord's questions was too much to cope with.

The patient's demeanor suddenly changed—her speech pattern, her stance, and even the way she addressed her therapist. Eve's posture became rigid, and she appeared to gain confidence. The person standing before Dr. Lord was very different from the patient who walked into his office less than an hour before. "Please address me by my name," she said forcefully.

"What should I call you?" Dr. Lord asked, trying not to sound condescending.

"My name is Dr. D, or you may call me Dr. Di Angelo."

Faced with the prospect of his patient being in the middle of a psychotic break, Dr. Lord tried not to agitate her. "Tell me, Dr. D, what are you feeling right now?"

Eve seemed unaware of her surroundings. She refused to answer but simply stared at the therapist. "How do you feel? Would you say you are scared?" It was obvious the previous line of questioning triggered Eve's use of defense mechanisms, but Dr. Lord would not give up on her.

Eve maintained a somewhat-combative stance and refused to answer Dr. Lord's questions. She stood up and threatened to walk out of the office but changed her mind when he prompted her to relax. "Eve, please take a deep breath and let us talk about whatever you like. Let's count backward from ten." She began the count down while taking deep breaths. "You are doing great. Close your eyes and imagine the sound of water trickling down. You feel relax and ready to meet me back in the office. Now open your eyes and take another deep breath." Dr. Lord made sure his client felt safe before moving forward.

Dr. D reassured his patient that he would go at her pace and meet her at her lowest point. "If you prefer to be called by a name other than Eve, I will do that. What should I call you?"

"My name is Dr. Mary Di Angelo," she repeated. "Who are you?"

It was obvious the patient was disconnected from reality. "Well, Dr. Mary Di Angelo, I am the person who has been walking with you through this journey." Eve stopped and lifted her hands in front of her face. She looked at them as if she was seeing them for the first time. "Eve, what are your thinking?" Dr. Lord gently reached out his hand and took Eve's. "It must be confusing to have so many different emotions surface at once." The conversation took on a different tone. The two began to talk with one-liners but understood the essence of the conversation without saying much.

EVE. *I'm scared.*
DR. LORD. *What scares you?*
EVE. *I don't know.*
DR. LORD. *I will walk with you.*
EVE. *How can I be sure?*
DR. LORD. *Have faith.*
EVE. *I'm scared.*
DR. LORD. *I know.*
DR. LORD. *Fear is not the absence of courage. It is a reminder that although you are not exempt from the perils of the world, you have a strength within that brings you through. Would you say that it could be a good thing?*
EVE. *What do you mean a good thing?*
DR. LORD. *Do you believe in someone greater than you?*
EVE. *I am not sure. My parents took me to church, and they believed in God.*
DR. LORD. *What do you believe?*
EVE. *I am not sure. I remember going to Sunday school.*
EVE. *I am scared.*

Eve suddenly stopped the volley of words between her and the doctor, perhaps to regain control of her emotions. Sensing his client's employment of a potentially negative defense mechanism, Dr. Lord decided to have Eve recall safer memories. "What did you like about Sunday school?"

Eve's eyes lit up and managed to allow a smile to glide across her face. "I remember Ms. Joanne. She was so kind and loving. She would have us memorize a new Bible verse every Sunday. If we got it right, she gave us a treat."

"Sounds like fond memories, Eve." Dr. Lord quickly followed up with a question. "Do you remember the Bible verse you said you often repeated as a child?"

Surprised by the question, it took Eve a second to respond. "Which Bible verse?"

Dr. Lord recited the following Bible verse, "Yea though I walk through the valley of the shadow of death, I will fear no evil; for thou art with me; thy rod and thy staff they comfort me."

A smile came over Eve's face, and she said, "Psalm 23, verse 4."

"Yes, Eve, it is Psalm 23."

"How did you know?"

"You shared that story with me before," Dr. Lord responded. Eve did not recall telling Dr. Lord about the Bible verse but was happy to hear it again. "I remember repeating it over and over."

"You did well," Dr. Lord responded like a proud parent but quickly reverted to a more therapeutic approach. "What did that verse mean to you? Why did you repeat it over and over?"

Eve did not get a chance to respond to Dr. Lord's question because a strong force seemed to draw her from one realm to another.

"Good morning, Eve." A cheery voice interrupted Eve's dream-state. "Are you okay? You are normally up and dressed early." Groggy and confused, Eve lifted her head from the pillow and asked the nurse how late it was. "You slept through breakfast, it's twelve o'clock in the afternoon."

"What! Why was I allowed to sleep so long?"

"We felt you needed extra rest." The nurse checked Eve's vital signs which were normal and reminded her that she had a 2:00-p.m. appointment with the psychiatrist. "I thought my appointment was 10 a.m.?"

"I think it was changed when the morning nurse saw how tired you appeared."

"Okay, thanks."

The next two hours prior to her appointment, Eve meditated on the voice in the dream. She recalled dreaming that she walked to a tiny room across the hall for her appointment with Dr. Lord. It was strange since she normally went to his office on the seventh floor. In the dream, she was escorted by a helper she did not recognize. This mystery helper wore a long shimmery dress-like outfit. It was hard to determine the person's gender—the figure was tall, thin, and almost translucent.

Eve stood in front of the bathroom mirror, trying her best to decipher what happened after she fell asleep. Still dazed from her encounter with the strange figure who escorted her to Dr. Lord's office, she wondered if the encounter was real. Eve remembered that her extraordinary meeting with Dr. Lord was short, and she barely recalled what was said. Still in a dream-like state, she blurted out, "Good night, Dr. Lord," while washing her face. Interestingly her meditation evolved into a full-blown conversation with the mysterious escort from the night before.

MYSTERIOUS ESCORT. Do you remember mumbling good night to Dr. Lord before you shuffled back to your room?

EVE. I don't remember doing that.

MYSTERIOUS ESCORT. I escorted you to your room and tried my best to engage you in conversation. My attempts to connect with you seemed futile, remember? We walked in complete silence.

EVE. Who are you? What do you want from me?

MYSTERIOUS ESCORT. Why do you think I want something from you? Maybe I came to give you something?

EVE. Why would you want to give me something? You don't know me.

MYSTERIOUS ESCORT. Eve, I know you very well. I know you want love and companionship like most people. I also know that you find it hard to trust people.

EVE. It's no mystery, most people want love and companionship.

MYSTERIOUS ESCORT. That is true. How many people fabricate that companionship?

EVE. What do you mean? I've never fabricated anything. In fact, I don't appreciate you saying that.

MYSTERIOUS ESCORT. Tell me about your husband John.

Before Eve was able to respond to the mysterious escort, Maria's voice interrupted the conversation, jolting her thoughts back to the reality of her room. "Hurry, Eve, it's almost time for your appointment."

"I-I-I'll be ready in a minute," Eve stuttered as she looked around and hurriedly brushed her hair into a messy bun. Obviously perplexed and intrigued by the conversation with the mysterious figure, Eve became a little annoyed by the interruption. "I wish I knew what he meant by fabricating," Eve murmured aloud, getting Maria's attention.

"What are you talking about?"

"Nothing, I am just thinking out loud."

Maria walked out of the room but soon returned to escort Eve, one of her favorite patients, up to her appointment on the seventh floor. "Sooo, how was your night?" Maria asked Eve in a playful tone. "I heard that you had a great day after your appointment with Dr. Lord." Still groggy but pensive, Eve responded with a nod. It almost seemed as if Eve had returned to the catatonic-like state that marked her interaction with others on the ward.

"Eve, are you listening to me?" Maria inquired, trying to ignite the spark Eve showed the day before. "You appeared so happy yesterday, at least that's what I was told."

Finally Eve spoke up, "I'm just thinking."

"What are you thinking about?"

"Well, last night I had a dream—at least, I think it was a dream."

Curious to know what the dream was but cautious not to shut off communication, Maria waited a few seconds before asking about the dream. Fortunately she did not have to wait long because Eve appeared eager to share. "Last night, I dreamt that I had a meeting with Dr. Lord. I was escorted to his office which was located on this floor. The weird thing is that I was escorted by someone I did not recognize. It was not Angel nor you. The person looked strange, like I could almost see through him or maybe her. I could not tell if it was a man or a woman. The figure was almost translucent, and I don't recall him talking—at least not with his mouth."

Maria listened intently as Eve recounted her experience. "Eve, do you mean that the figure may have had a conversation but not a verbal one?"

Eve must have realized that Maria was having a difficult time digesting the dream. "Well…Maybe in dreams, it is hard to tell when someone is talking to you."

"I see," Maria responded, still grappling to understand the strange dream.

Eve quickly interrupted the silence. "My conversation with Dr. Lord seemed strange."

"What do you mean?"

"He did not seem to be my doctor. I felt like he was more." In an attempt to re-establish the therapeutic boundaries, Maria reminded Eve that psychiatrist, therapist, counselors sometimes have such a strong bond with their clients, it may seem like they are family member or a friend.

"Remember you came to us in a very vulnerable state, and the staff and Dr. Lord became your support system. It does not mean that Dr. Lord is more than your psychiatrist." Maria was a quick study. She was finally learning about boundaries and helping clients to remain grounded.

During Maria's short monologue about therapeutic boundaries, Eve remained silent but pensive. "I don't think I saw Dr. Lord as a friend or family member. When I say that he was more, I mean some type of higher power."

Maria jumped in with a plausible explanation. "When a patient is very ill or feeling vulnerable, his or her doctor may seem larger than life." Her explanation did not hit home with her patient who seemed frustrated by Maria's attempts to psychoanalyze the situation.

Finally frustrated, Eve conceded to Maria's explanation. "Maybe you are right."

The elevator ride was marked by complete silence following the earlier exchange that left Eve feeling frustrated. Neither Maria nor Eve said a word and barely looked at each other. "Here we are!" Maria exclaimed in an attempt to break the ice before walking up to Dr.

Lord's receptionist. "Hi, I brought Eve for her appointment with Dr. Lord."

The receptionist asked the pair to take a seat in the waiting room. "Are you okay? I hope I did not upset you. Maria's concern for her patient led her to ask even more questions which continued to irritate Eve.

"Maria, I am okay. If I need to talk with someone, I can talk to Dr. Lord." Eve's response clearly indicated that she was not in the mood to continue the conversation with Maria.

Third Session with Dr. Lord

The receptionist signaled to Eve that Dr. Lord was ready to see her. As Eve entered the room, she noticed a few changes but did not say anything at that time. "Hello, Dr. Lord, how are you?"

"I am well, Eve, how are you?"

"I am doing okay, Dr. Lord." It was obvious she had something on her mind. Instead Eve focused on the changes in the office. "I didn't notice the wingback chair in the corner before," Eve said with somewhat of an attitude.

"Do you like it?" Dr. Lord asked.

"I guess," Eve responded as her voice trailed.

"Sounds like you have more to say about the chair."

"It reminds me of the chair I had in my office."

"Oh!" Dr. Lord exclaimed but did not follow up on Eve's statement.

Both doctor and patient chose to ignore the previous exchange, opting to talk about more mundane issues. The session was uneventful; Dr. Lord asked questions, and Eve responded. She seemed preoccupied but tried her best to be present. Suddenly Eve posed a question that, on the surface, seemed to catch Dr. Lord by surprise. "Do you believe in God?"

Eve's question was mirrored by the same question from Dr. Lord. "Do you believe in God?"

Eve appeared to ponder the question for a few seconds before responding. "I believe there is a God, but I don't understand him."

"What would you like to understand?" Dr. Lord asked, but Eve did not answer the question.

"I remember the Bible verse that states, 'So God so loved the world that he gave his only son, that whosoever believes in him shall not perish but have eternal life' (John 3:16). Well, if he loves us, why does bad things happen to good people?"

"Great question!" Dr. Lord exclaimed and followed up by comparing God's love to the love of a father toward a disobedient child. "Parents love their children but are unable to protect them when they choose to walk away from the shelter and security of the parent's arms. What do you think about the analogy, Eve?"

"I am not sure. Is the session almost over?"

Sensing Eve's discomfort, Dr. Lord decided to end the session and pick up the conversation during their next session. "It's obvious that you need more time to think about the analogy. What do you think about continuing our dialogue tomorrow? The brake might be good for you."

Dr. Lord rang the receptionist and told her to have one of the nurses come up to the seventh floor to get Eve. "A nurse should be here shortly to escort you back to your floor. Are you okay sitting in the waiting room until someone comes?"

Eve slowly walked to the reception area where she sat and stared at the wall. Her thoughts flashed back to the dream—particularly her conversation with Dr. Lord. Surprisingly, Eve chose not to discuss her dream with Dr. Lord. A million thoughts swirled in her head but not one thought about discussing her dream with her doctor.

Eve was so distracted by her thoughts, she did not see Maria get off the elevator. "How was your appointment?" Maria asked, anticipating a detailed description of the session. Unfortunately she would be disappointed by the unceremonious response from Eve.

"It was okay."

"Are you ready to return to your room?" Eve nodded and walked silently to the elevator. "I am surprised that your appointment ended so quickly. Were you able to talk to Dr. Lord about your dream?"

"No, I did not get a chance to talk about it."

"I am surprised, you seemed enthusiastic about the prospect of talking to Dr. Lord about it." Eve did not respond, she simply walked ahead of Maria to catch the elevator. The elevator ride from the seventh to the fourth floor seemed longer than usual, perhaps because of the palpable tension. "Eve…Eve, we are here." The patient looked at Maria and stepped off the elevator without saying a word.

"Did Dr. Lord tell you what time is your next appointment?" Maria asked even though she knew the answer to the question. Her attempt to initiate a dialogue with Eve and perhaps glean information about the session was futile.

"No, I don't know when my next appointment will be." Eve erected a wall between her and the nurse. She often did so when she felt vulnerable. "No, I don't know when my next appointment will be." She turned her back to Maria, walked into the room, and sat on the bed facing the wall. Her behavior reminded Maria of a five-year-old throwing a tantrum. Eve stared at the wall for at least thirty minutes before falling asleep.

Maria watched her intently, still trying to understand the complex nature of Eve's behavior. She asked Angel, the psych tech, about Eve's mood the day before. "Angel, I am concerned that Eve might be spiraling into a major depression. What do you think?" Angel did not seem too worried but told Maria that the staff were also concerned about Eve's apparent lack of stability.

It was not long before Eve fell into a deep sleep. "Eve," she heard a faint voice call out in the night. "Can you hear me, Eve?" The voice continued to echo in the room.

Finally Eve answered but did not readily recognize the voice of the person calling her. "I am awake, what do you want with me?"

"You know!" The voice asserted before a deafening silence filled the room.

"I don't know what you want," Eve protested, this time, opening her eyes to ascertain who was behind the voice. Once again, the voice repeated the assertion that Eve knew what he wanted. Unfortunately Eve did not seem to know. Baffled, Eve looked around the room, trying to orient herself. Before Eve was able to respond, she heard, "Just follow me."

Eve jumped out of the bed and followed the voice to a tiny room across the hall where she sat on the edge of a chair near the entrance. Her hands carefully placed on her lap like a soldier sitting at attention with perfect posture, ready to follow commands.

"Hello, Eve, how are you?"

"Dr. Lord, what are you doing here?"

"I'm here for our meeting, don't you remember?"

Surprised and confused, Eve looked around before addressing her psychiatrist. She repeated her question. "What are you doing here? I thought our appointment was tomorrow afternoon sometime."

"You called me."

"When did I call you?" Eve protested, looking around, trying to figure out what was happening. "The last thing I remember was sitting on the bed, staring at the wall before falling asleep, I think."

Eve had barely completed her sentence before Dr. Lord chimed in. "Tell me something, what did you mean when you said, 'Lord, I don't understand?'" He promptly followed his first question with another. "What don't you understand?" Concerned that he might have been too pushy, he softened his tone. "You seemed a little confused by the question."

Eve sighed and leaned forward in the chair. Following what seemed to be an eternity, she looked at the doctor and said, "I wish I could see John, maybe touch his hand and feel his breath as he tells me how much he loves me. I miss feeling the steady beat of his heart."

Surprised by her statement which seemed to come out of nowhere, Dr. Lord shook his head affirmatively and said, "I bet you miss your husband."

"Why did he die? I don't understand."

"I know I asked this before but tell me more about John. How old was he, where did you meet him, and how long were you married?"

Unexpectedly a figure appeared in the shadows and stood without saying a word. "Who are you? Wait a minute—John?" Eve stood up and took a step toward the figure but stopped short of touching him. "Is that really you? How can this be?" Eve looked at Dr. Lord as if asking for his permission to approach the figure. As she took another step forward, the look in her eyes made it obvious she had a million questions swirling in her head. Eve stared at the figure as she reached out with trepidation to touch him—the love of her life.

"Eve, tell me about John." Dr. Lord's voice interrupted the encounter and immediately, the figure disappeared.

"No, no, no! What did you do, Dr. Lord? He is gone, why did you make him disappear? Please bring him back again." Eve's cries were simply met by a question.

"Tell me about John."

Almost immediately, Eve quieted her sobbing and looked at the psychiatrist. "I love him, and I miss him."

Dr. Lord quickly asserted, "I asked you to tell me about him, not what you felt about him."

Surprised by Dr. Lord's forceful response yet undeterred, Eve said, "He is kind, loving, and patient. I could always talk to him without feeling judged. He never made me feel foolish or insignificant." Her voice trailed but picked up strength again. "John never focused on himself. His aim was always to please me. I always looked forward to coming home from work because he kept my food warm and an open ear for my stories. You know, he liked my stories. John did not even mind my dog, Casper, jumping on the sofa or the bed."

"John sounds like the perfect man." Dr. Lord briefly interrupted but allowed his patient to continue.

"John loved me and wanted to please me. I really miss having someone who understood me and was willing to do whatever it took to make me happy."

"If John were here, what would you say to him?"

"I would tell him how much I love him and miss him. He supported my passion to help others who suffered from mental illness or just…" Her voice got softer.

"Just what?" Dr. Lord inquired, trying to get Eve to finish the sentence.

She took a deep breath before going on. "He supported what I did to help people who felt that they were missing a vital piece of life."

"Tell me about some of the people you helped along the way."

Eve's eyes become heavy, and she started slurring her words. "I am feeling very sleepy. I am not sure why. Maybe we can continue this conversation at our next appointment."

It was obvious to Dr. Lord that the patient was avoiding a conversation that might open the door to unexplored issues. "Thank you for sharing your feelings about John, maybe next time you might share details about this person who you love and honor." Eve did not respond to her doctor. She did not even acknowledge hearing what Dr. Lord said.

Again Eve felt a pull away from her conversation with Dr. Lord. "Hey, sleepyhead. You overslept. I have been trying to wake you up for the last few minutes. You must be extremely tired." Maria wondered if her patient was experiencing insomnia because of some deep-seated emotional issue being dug up in therapy. "Are you having trouble sleeping because of your sessions with Dr. Lord?" Maria asked in her best nonjudgmental tone.

However, Eve did not respond to the question because she was groggy. "I will be ready in a few minutes to go to my appointment." The thought of last night's dream still haunted her; yet she did not share the dream with Maria.

"No rush, you still have twenty minutes—maybe thirty minutes tops—before your appointment."

Groggy and still disoriented, Eve walked slowly toward the bathroom before stopping to take a deep breath. If felt as if she was walking into the tiny room across the hall; perhaps she would have another encounter with John. "I wish I could see you again, John." Eve said to herself as she picked up her toothbrush and slowly put the toothpaste on it. "Did I actually see John, or was it just a vivid dream?" It was becoming difficult to differentiate between her dreams and time spent with Dr. Lord. The whole encounter seemed so real. Eve began to think, perhaps she was losing her mind.

"Ready!" A few minutes later Maria poked her head in the room to encourage her patient to hurry. Maria realized that Eve had not eaten breakfast and asked if she would like to get a bite to eat before heading to the seventh floor.

"I am not real hungry. I think I'll wait until after my appointment to have a bite to eat."

Just as Maria got ready to walk out the room, she heard Eve say, "I am ready to go, Maria. This is my fourth session with Dr. Lord, and I feel a little scared."

Surprised by Eve's assertion, Maria tried to reassure her patient at the same time, she inquired about the nature of Eve's fear. "Dr. Lord is gentle and will not allow anything to harm you."

"I know," Eve responded with obvious tension in her voice.

However, Maria continued to press for a reason. "Can you tell me why you are scared? This is not your first time seeing Dr. Lord."

"I don't know." Eve evaded the question. Instead she asked Maria about her day. "How is your day so far, Maria?" Sensing that her patient did not want to talk about her feelings, Maria obliged Eve's desire to avoid the conversation.

The two women walked in silence toward the elevator but ended the uncomfortable silence when they almost bumped into each other trying to get on the elevator. "Sorry," Eve said as she tried to avoid running into Maria.

Both laughed as they simultaneously said, "Want to dance?" Both women got on the elevator and returned to the silence that previously punctuated the walk to the elevator.

"Here we are. Are you ready to talk to Dr. Lord?" Maria made a last-ditch effort to get some information from Eve.

"I think so." For some strange reason, Maria decided stop asking anymore questions.

"Okay." Maria was unable to explain the strong force that compelled her to back off.

"Hello, Eve, welcome back. How are you feeling?" Dr. Lord's receptionist welcomed Eve before having her take a seat in the waiting room.

"Please call me when Eve is done seeing Dr. Lord. The patient is not feeling well, she didn't sleep well last night." Maria cautioned the receptionist before heading toward the elevator. "I will see you shortly," she told Eve just before getting on the elevator.

"Eve," the receptionist called twice before Eve responded. "Dr. Lord is ready to see you."

Eve got up and walked slowly to Dr. Lord's office. She appeared lethargic and preoccupied by her thoughts. "Nice seeing you, Eve," the receptionist said, attempting to engage her, to no avail.

"Hello, Eve, come on in," Dr. Lord greeted Eve at the door. Eve looked at him and said hello before taking a seat on the chair near the door.

"How are you doing?" Dr. Lord dove right in, skipping the pleasantries.

"I am doing okay," Eve responded in a monotone voice.

"You seem tired."

"I am a little tired because I did not sleep well last night."

"Want to talk about it?"

"Well…I do want to talk about it, but I am not sure how to start."

"Just start from the beginning." Dr. Lord prompted his patient to dive into session.

"Do you believe that dreams reveal what is going on inside of us?"

"It depends. That's a very insightful question, Eve." Dr. Lord was purposefully vague to encourage a dialogue with his patient. "What do you think, Eve?"

"I think that our dreams sometimes reveal events that are happening in another realm. Kind of like a spiritual realm." Eve clarified her statement before she continued sharing her concerns. "Sometimes dreams seem so real. It's hard for me to decipher when it is a dream or reality."

"That is true, Eve. Some dreams seem so real it is difficult to determine if we are awake or sleeping. I bet you must feel confused."

"I am not sure if I was dreaming last night, but I had a peculiar encounter. I remember sitting on my bed but do not recall falling asleep. The next thing I remember was hearing your voice."

"My voice?" Dr. Lord asked but did not comment further.

"Yes, it was strange. This is not the first time I thought I heard your voice in my dreams. Last night, I got up and followed the voice to a small office across the hall. You were there, and we talked. You asked me a few questions about John. That was when something strange happened."

Eve stopped for a moment and wiped a tear from her eye. This was very unusual for this patient. She hardly ever showed emotions. In fact, Dr. Lord was surprised and brought it to her attention. "Eve, it is a pleasant surprise to see you show emotions."

"What are you thinking about?" She looked at the psychiatrist for a few seconds before responding. "I feel sad. It has been a long time since I have felt anything."

"What do you think is bringing these feelings to the surface?"

"I think the vivid dreams I am having…" Her voice trailed, and she stared into space for a few seconds before finishing the sentence. "I think the dreams are making me feel emotions that I have not felt in a long time."

Eve continued recounting her experience. "I saw John in my dream last night. At least, I think I was dreaming. It seemed so real."

"Dr. Lord, I heard your voice and followed it to a tiny office across from my room," Eve said to the psychiatrist. "When I walked into the office, we talked and suddenly, John appeared. I was elated, but it did not last very long because he disappeared."

"What happened?" Dr. Lord asked.

"He unexpectedly disappeared when you interrupted my attempts to touch him."

"Why do you think he disappeared?" Dr. Lord inquired as he leaned forward in his chair.

"I don't know," Eve replied, looking very sad. "I remember talking to him, and I tried moving closer." She paused. "When I reached out to touch him, he was gone. It was as if I was looking at a mirage. Does that make sense?"

"A mirage?" Dr. Lord repeated.

"Yes, you know, like seeing water in the desert, but it is not real." Dr. Lord did not tell his patient that he knew what a mirage was but wanted her to reflect on the experience.

"How did you feel when you saw John?"

"I was happy when I saw him but felt very sad when he disappeared. He looked so real, but he did not speak to me. Strange, I don't remember the sound of his voice. In fact, it took some effort on my part to recognize John." Eve stopped and looked at her hands as she held them in a prayer position. She slowly scanned the room before fixing her eyes on a picture on the wall. It was apparent she was thinking about John. She made an unintelligible sound and placed her hand on her head. "Aha." She uttered as someone who got the answer to a serious question. Her eyes moved away from the picture and landed on Dr. Lord. She did not speak right away. “I feel conflicted.”

“Go on.” Dr. Lord prompted her.

“There is a part of me that felt angry when I saw John, but I don’t understand why.”

“Sometimes we have unresolved feelings that lay dormant until we feel safe enough to express them. Do you feel safe?” Dr. Lord asked Eve to trust him and the safety of his office. For the first time since beginning therapy with Dr. Lord, Eve seemed willing to open up and talk about her feelings. Unfortunately it was not to happen during that session. Eve began to rock back and forth and asked if she could go back to the room. Dr. Lord perceived that he touched on something significant but felt it was best to end the session. He asked the receptionist to contact someone on the fourth floor to escort his patient.

“Hi, Maria, this is Dr. Lord’s receptionist. Eve is ready to go back to her room.”

Another unfruitful session or was it? Eve seemed defeated as she walked out of the office, but the receptionist’s smile always seemed to lift her spirit. “Eve, you may sit in the waiting room until Maria is able to pick you up,” Esperanza said with a smile and a wink which brought a smile to the patient’s countenance. Eve returned the wink before heading to the waiting room. She sat down but instead of staring at the ground as she usually did, Eve picked up a magazine from the table next to her chair. Drawn by an article about relationships, she opened the magazine and started reading. For the first time since being admitted, Eve seemed interested in something outside her own world.

Her curiosity in the article did not last long because a familiar voice drew her attention away from the magazine. “Hi, Eve, are you ready to go back to your room?” It was Maria; she seemed hurried when she stepped off the elevator. She skipped her usual salutation and questions. “Are you ready?” Maria repeated forcefully. Eve placed the magazine where she found it and got up slowly from her seat.

Her demeanor gave the impression she was not ready to go back to the room. However, she got up from her seat and followed the nurse.

"Hold the elevator," Maria shouted to one of the workers. She ran toward the elevator while Eve walked slowly behind her. "Thank you," Maria said to the worker who held the door.

"Here we are, fourth floor," Maria announced as she reached out her hand to help Eve off the elevator. Initially neither said a word as they walked toward the room. "Eve, are you okay?" Maria finally spoke but did not wait for an answer. She picked up Eve's chart at the nurse's station and took her vitals. "Everything looks okay, your blood pressure is great. Let me know if you need anything." Maria seemed aloof but very professional. Eve was in no condition to notice the difference. She had just experienced a therapeutic breakthrough which appeared to set her back emotionally.

Eve did not linger at the station. She went in to her room and took out a tablet from the nightstand next to her bed. She sat at the edge of the bed and began writing. She was so engrossed in her writing, she did not notice Angel standing at the door, knocking. "Hi, Eve, are you ready for your meds?" The psychiatric technician walked in and placed the medication tray on the desk. "I know your night meds make you sleepy, and you may not be ready to go to bed. If you like, I can come back a little later."

"Yes, please," Eve said without looking up. "I would like to have at least another hour to write."

"I can come back in half an hour. I am sorry that I cannot accommodate you, but the doctor wants you to take the meds no later than 9:00 p.m."

"Okay, I will take them in thirty minutes."

Eve continued writing and thinking. She occasionally looked at the clock to see if the thirty minutes had passed. Captivated by the writing in her journal, she did not notice that time had flown.

"Hi, Eve, I am back with your medication. Are you ready to take them?" Eve was not ready but knew she had to take her meds. Angel waited to make sure Eve took her medication before walking back to the nurse's station. After taking the medication, Eve continued feverishly writing like someone on a mission. Soon her eyes became heavy, and she could no longer see the writing on the page. "I think I am going to stop here and resume tomorrow." Eve told herself as she closed the notebook. It was not long before she began to dose off.

Another Dream State

"Eve, can you hear me?" The voice beckoned her to rise from her bed and go to the rendezvous point.

"Yes, I hear you." This time, Eve responded and immediately got out of her bed and followed the voice.

"Welcome, Eve," a voice as deep as the deepest waters greeted her.

"Dr. Lord?" Eve said, almost as if she was asking a question. This time, the tiny room looked different. The chair by the door was no longer there. In its place, there was a rocking chair like the one she had in her room when she was a child. In fact, the room reminded her of the tiny apartment she grew up in. Confused, she asked Dr. Lord for an explanation. "Why does the room look like the apartment I grew up in?"

Dr. Lord looked at Eve but did not answer. Instead the psychiatrist motioned to Eve to sit on the rocking chair. Before Eve could sit on the chair, she had a flashback of her mother telling the story about Jonah in the belly of the big fish. The vision did not scare her. Eve sat on the chair and rocked back and forth as she hugged herself.

Suddenly the patient let out a deafening and unexpected scream that would rival a scream from a scary Hollywood movie. Dr. Lord did not move; in fact, he did not seem bothered by her scream.

"Mom, where is Daddy?" Like a frightened child, Eve asked for her dad over and over before Dr. Lord intervened.

"Eve, take a deep breath. I want you to look at me and continue to breathe deeply."

Finally Eve calmed down enough to stop screaming. She also stopped asking for her dad. Dr. Lord did not appear to be moved by Eve's distress. "What is going through your mind right now?" Dr. Lord asked in a very calm tone.

"I don't know," Eve responded, still shaking and rocking.

"Let's do our grounding exercise." Dr. Lord's intervened. "I want you to inhale deeply through your nose and exhale through your mouth. I will ask you some questions, and I want you to respond with a brief phrase or sentence. We will then play a word game. I will say a word, and you tell me what comes to mind." Eve nodded, and Dr. Lord began the exercise.

DR. LORD. *I want you to say your full name.*
EVE. *My name is Eve Di Angelo.*
DR. LORD. *How old are you, Eve?*
EVE. *I am…I think I am thirty-five or maybe forty years old.*
She appeared confused and could not remember her age.
DR. LORD. *Take a deep breath as you close your eyes.*
EVE. *Breathes deeply.*
DR. LORD. *I want you to focus your attention on the breath, count the number of inhales and exhales.*
EVE. *One, two, three, four, five.*
DR. LORD. *Can you feel the floor under your feet?*
EVE. *Yes.*
DR. LORD. *Stop and listen to the sounds around you. What do you hear?*
EVE. *I hear quietness.*
DR. LORD. *What else do you hear?*
EVE. *I hear your voice.*
DR. LORD. *Take another deep breath and when you are ready, I want you to open your eyes.*
EVE. *Ahh.*

The patient took another deep breath before opening her eyes.

DR. LORD. *Now I will give you a series of words and would like you to respond with a word, thought, or phrase.*
DR. LORD. *Love*
EVE. *John*
DR. LORD. *Pain*
EVE. *John*
DR. LORD. *Safety*

EVE. I don't know.
DR. LORD. How do you define safety?
EVE. The absence of fear
DR. LORD. Fear
EVE. I don't know.

Dr. Lord noticed Eve's dichotomous response about John but did not address it. "I feel a little better. Thank you, Dr. Lord," Eve said in an attempt to avoid answering more questions. She appeared calmer and ready to talk about her feelings, although she did not want to continue with the grounding exercise. Without prompting, Eve started talking about her experience sitting in the rocking chair. "I felt myself return to the tiny apartment where I grew up. I was sitting in the rocking chair, hearing my mom tell me the story about Jonah being swallowed by the big fish." Then her voice trailed.

"What happened?" Dr. Lord asked as he reassured her with a pat on her arm.

"I don't remember anything else."

"You don't remember or don't want to talk about it?"

Eve continued to rock back and forth with her hands wrapped around her body. "I guess I don't want to talk about it just yet," she responded without further explanation.

"It is hard to address bad memories." Dr. Lord recognized that the patient might have gotten in touch with something traumatic and was not ready to discuss it. "Eve, would you like to continue talking about your experience in the rocking chair?"

Eve paused for a few seconds before responding. "I think I would like to end the session."

"How are you feeling?" Dr. Lord asked, concerned about his patient.

"I think I am okay, but I don't want to continue."

"You did very well, Eve," Dr. Lord reassured her.

"Eve, are you awake?" As in the previous dream-state, it was hard to tell the difference between fantasy and reality. The voice became louder before she realized it was the voice of one of the nurses. "Eve, wake up. It's time for breakfast."

She sat straight up in the bed, appearing less groggy than the previous night. "I am up, and I am hungry," she said to the nurse as she rubbed her stomach.

"I think you will like what's on today's menu. They have pancakes, egg, and ham."

"Yummy," Eve responded as she rubbed her hands together, indicating that she was eager to dig in.

Eve was not scheduled for her therapy session until later that day. She had the entire morning to think about her dream-state visit with Dr. Lord. This time, she was not anxious, sad, or fearful about what transpired the night before. Although her dream-state session was profound, she was in an upbeat mood. She did not even have a conversation with her mysterious escort like she had after previous encounters. "Eve, the other patients are going to play bingo in the recreation room in an hour. Would you like to join them?" The charge nurse asked as she hurried by with a clipboard in her hand.

"I think I will do some writing, I am not feeling very social," Eve responded to the nurse as she combed her hair.

Eve continued grooming while some of the nurses busily went about their morning routines. The charge nurse barked orders while the other nurses took the patients' temperature or checked their blood pressure. The scene seemed like controlled chaos. The confusion did not seem to bother Eve. She was upbeat and smiling, looking forward to her meeting with Dr. Lord. After one of the nurses took her blood pressure, she decided to walk over to the nurses' station across from her room to check on the details of her appointment. She almost had a skip in her step—unusual for Eve.

"Maria, are you escorting me to my appointment today?"

"I am not sure who will take you, either myself or Angel will come and get you ten minutes before your session. Everyone is busy today, therefore, we have to share all tasks," Maria talked as she shuffled some papers on the desk. "Don't worry, Eve, I will let you know who is going to escort you, give me at least thirty minutes."

Eve went back to her room and opened her journal but instead of writing, she began to read some of her notes. It was as if she read them for the first time. She seemed mesmerized by the content of the notebook. Every page elicited a new emotion and revealed a fresh perspective. Eve lost herself in the pages of her notebook and also lost track of time.

"Eve, are you ready?" Maria peeked in the room to let her know that she was ready to escort her.

"Oh, it's time already?" Eve was so preoccupied with her notes that she did not notice the time. "I am ready to go," Eve said as she gathered her notepad and put on a sweater since it was a bit nippy. The nurses had no control over the thermostat, so the ward was a little chilly.

"Come on, Eve, we are running a little behind. Dr. Lord is waiting on you."

"We are only going to the seventh floor, not across the state." Maria said jokingly to which Eve protested but hurried to catch up.

Fourth Session with Dr. Lord

"Hello, Eve, how are you today?" Dr. Lord's receptionist welcomed their patient with a smile.

"I am doing well. How are you?"

"I can't complain. It's been a long day but seeing you brought a smile to my face." For the first time, Eve and the receptionist interacted beyond a simple notification that Dr. Lord was ready to see her. Eve sat in the waiting area for a few seconds before Dr. Lord appeared. "How are you, Eve? Come in and have a seat," Dr. Lord greeted his patient who seemed eager to get started.

She settled in on the green wingback chair across from her psychiatrist and uncovered a notebook she had concealed under her robe. "What do you have there?" Curious, Dr. Lord inquired about the notebook.

"It's just a notebook I use to record my thoughts."

"You mean like a journal?"

"Not really a journal, more like a dream book."

"Anything you are comfortable sharing?" Dr. Lord asked with some trepidation but reminded his patient that it was her choice to share the content of the notebook. "Feel free to take the lead."

Without further prompting from Dr. Lord, Eve opened the notebook and began to read some of the thoughts she recorded over the past few days. "Last night was difficult for me. I thought about my life in general terms and wondered what happened. I don't know how I ended up here, but I think I am ready to find out." Eve took a deep breath and continued reading. "Recently I have been dreaming about my therapy sessions. At least, I think they are dreams. Sometimes I feel as if I am awake, and my dreams are occurring in real life." She stopped and looked at Dr. Lord as if she needed help with the next sentence. "Dr. Lord, have you ever had a dream that feels real? I mean, it feels as if you are actually experiencing whatever you are dreaming about." Eve had a difficult time expressing her thoughts, so she tried to use an example instead of waiting for Dr. Lord to respond to her question. "For example, the last few nights, I felt as if I met you in a tiny office across from my room. It did not feel like a dream. In fact, you sent someone to escort me to the room. Some nights, I actually hear you calling me. Does that seem weird?"

Dr. Lord listened patiently as Eve described her experience. However, during a brief period of silence, he inquired about Eve's last comment. "You said that you heard my voice calling you. What do you make of it?"

"I am not sure," Eve responded but followed up with a question of her own. "Do you believe in God?"

Dr. Lord smiled. He did not seem surprised by the question. Instead of answering Eve's question, he asked another question. Both seemed caught up in a game of chess. "Why do you ask?"

"I don't know. I guess I have questions about the existence of a deity."

"What types of questions?"

"For starters, does God exist?"

"Can you answer that question?" Dr. Lord answered her question by posing yet another question. "Do you believe that God exists?"

"I don't know but if he did, I don't think he would allow children to suffer."

Eve seemed more willing to talk about her feelings than she did during the last few sessions. Strangely she appeared settled, ready to address the problems that kept her from experiencing life to the fullest. Who knows? She might be ready to deal with the issues that brought her to the hospital. This time she did not stop the session, walk out, or cried uncontrollably. In fact, she responded to Dr. Lord's questions and was not upset that he did not respond to hers.

"I did believe in God at some point in my life," Eve said. Dr. Lord nodded but did not say anything. Eve continued talking. "I am not sure exactly when that changed." Suddenly Eve's affect looked strained, and she became concerned with the time. "What time is it? How long have we been talking?" Dr. Lord was used to seeing his patient decompensate (have a meltdown) anytime she connected to negative emotions or simply was not ready or willing to continue the session.

"Eve, I think you have what it takes to push through the pain," Dr. Lord said softly as he leaned forward in his chair. He knew that with a little encouragement, his client might continue.

Eve gathered her thoughts and collected her notebook before continuing. "My mom was a believer. She taught me that God would take care of us no matter what. She went to church every Sunday and took me with her. My dad didn't go every Sunday but went on special holidays." Eve stopped and stared ahead as if recalling an event that took place a long time ago. "I enjoyed church especially Sunday school. I still remember my Sunday school teacher, Ms. Johnson. She was such a nice lady and cared for her students."

Dr. Lord didn't dare interrupt his patient. He simply allowed her to lead the therapy session. "I think she must have talked to my mom because they both enjoyed telling the same Bible story." Eve laughed nervously and took a deep breath, perhaps an indication that the memory was pleasant. "I remember inviting my friend Mary to church, but she did not like going. She went with me two times but never went back." Eve paused before going on. "I often wished my mom gave me the freedom to choose. I envied Mary because her parents let her stay home from church. Now that I look back though, I am glad my mom made me go to church."

Dr. Lord interjected with a question. "Why do you say that?"

Eve shot back with a question. "What do you mean?"

Dr. Lord explained his question. "You stated that in retrospect, you were glad that your mom made you go to church."

"Yes, it helped me deal with many stressful situations."

"I see," Dr. Lord said as he nodded and leaned toward his client.

Finally Eve was able to relax and seemed willing to trust Dr. Lord with the secret locked inside her for many years. Doctor and patient had developed a rhythm that moved them closer to uncovering the reason for Eve's hospitalization. Unfortunately Eve did not reveal her secret during that session nor was she able to access the thoughts that haunted her and brought her to her psychiatrist. Dr. Lord did not give up; however, he continued to patiently allow Eve to walk slowly toward the hidden secret locked in the recesses of her mind. She got close many times during the fourth session but panicked and stepped back. The session ended, and Eve waited for someone to escort her to her room. This session was different, she seemed more relaxed and happy.

"The truth shall set your free! Isn't that what the Bible says?" Eve mumbled to herself as she left Dr. Lord's office. Unfortunately she did not appear ready to deal with the truth that might set her free.

Eve walked out of Dr. Lord's office and bumped into Maria who was waiting in the lobby. "Oh hi, Maria, how long have you been waiting?" Maria arrived on the seventh floor a little early to pick her up. She often enjoyed sitting in the waiting room because it was beautiful and peaceful.

"Are you ready to get back to the ward?" Maria asked, not certain she was ready to leave the beauty of the seventh floor.

"Yes, I am ready," Eve responded. The pair got on the elevator but did not talk on the ride down to the fourth floor. Eve seem to ponder her future while Maria thought about the work she still had left to do before leaving for the day.

"We are here!" Eve exclaimed as the elevator came to a stop. Back on the fourth floor, Eve walked to her room and sat on the edge of her bed. She reflected on her session with Dr. Lord while she entertained the thought of achieving freedom from her emotional prison. Flashes of memory took her back to the tiny apartment and the rocking chair where her mother sat and recounted story after story from the Bible. In her mind's eyes, she had a clear picture of her mother during happier times, rocking back and forth. The memories brought a smile to her face. Occasionally a memory of her dad would pop into her mind but did not seem to linger. She recalled her dad kissing her on the forehead before going to sleep which warmed her heart.

The memory flashes also conjured thoughts of darker times; she didn't remember exactly what happened but knew it was not pleasant. A fleeting thought came to her mind and interrupted the walk down memory lane. "Both bitter and sweet waters flowing into the same cistern. How is that possible?" she said under her breath. "Why did I say that?" Eve asked herself before sensing a familiar but dark presence in the room. It wasn't the first time she experienced this presence but this time, she believed she possessed an inner strength to overcome her fear. Resolute, Eve muttered, "Even if I don't have the strength to resist you, I no longer feel the urge to give into the darkness."

No longer terrified by the thought of losing control to the darkness that often enveloped her and clouded her thoughts, she decided it was time to fight back. Sadness ruled her world for many years. It robbed her of the ability to express herself and enjoy life's gifts. This time, she would use her pen as a weapon to dispel the gloom.

Eve took out her diary and started writing. She committed every thought to paper and tried to connect each segment of her story like a puzzle. Her past had become unmanageable, but her future suddenly seemed bright. Unable to complete the puzzle because of the missing piece, she had simply given up. However, there was renewed hope.

"This time, I will write until I locate the missing piece of my puzzle." She sighed and thought, *If I could just find the missing piece.* "Don't think that way, Eve. You will find the missing piece," Eve said audibly as she wrote in the notebook.

Each night in a dream-like state, she came closer and closer to finding the missing piece. Dr. Lord was helpful, but something kept her from fully trusting him. She realized that she was unwilling to trust anyone. "Why is he so kind?" Eve asked herself as she continued to document her thoughts. "What does he want from me? I don't think he wants anything," she asked the question and responded but continued to be plagued by doubt.

"Lights out." One of the nurses peeked inside the room and reminded Eve that it was almost bedtime. "Remember that you can use the reading lamp above the bed, but you must read quietly." The night-shift nurse reminded her of the rules. The overhead light was not allowed after a certain hour because it disturbed other patients. Eve did not seem bothered by the request; she happily complied and turned on the reading lamp. Eve continued writing about her feelings well into the night.

Her diary entries seemed to have changed. This entry was different than previous ones but as detailed as the entries in the notebook she brought with her to the hospital. "How could I face the fact that the patient was me?" Eve wrote. "The counselor becomes the counselee. I am dealing with my fragmented self. A double-minded person is unstable in all their ways." One confusing entry after another. Her thoughts reflected the perplexity of her world and her inability to make sense of it. Eve's last entry summarized her confusion. "Am I who I am supposed to be? A puzzle undone is how she sees herself." Her notes went on, seemingly disconnected and lacking rhyme or reason. Was Eve descending into a state of madness? Perhaps the disconnected thoughts in the notebook were a veiled attempt to reach the outside world. On the other hand, it could simply be an indication of insanity. Who knows!

Finally Eve's eyes became heavy, and she started yawning. "Try to stay awake one more hour," she told herself, to no avail. It was not long before she gave up and carefully placed the notebook in the drawer of the nightstand beside her bed. Eve said a quick prayer before getting under the covers. The last time she said a bedtime prayer, she was a kid. Somehow the last session elicited renewed faith—Eve longed to have confidence in something or someone.

"Eve, get up and follow me," once again, the familiar voice beckoned.

She opened her eyes and looked around before getting out of bed. "Who are you?" she asked as she got from under the covers and followed the voice. Soon Eve found herself by the doorway of a small room with a rocking chair. The room mirrored the tiny apartment she grew up in. "Hello, is anyone here?" she called out.

"Hello, Eve, come on in." Dr. Lord's voice thundered in the room but soothed his client. It is hard to explain the paradox. His voice, although deep, strong, and profound, brought Eve a sense of peace and comfort.

Eve walked into the room and sat on a rocking chair near the door. It reminded her of the one she sat in as a little girl to listen to her mom's Bible stories. It was not long after sitting on the chair, she began singing a song in an unknown language no one but she and Dr. Lord understood. The lyrics of the song were unfamiliar to Eve, but she sung as if she always knew the song. The words to the song remain a mystery until this day. Eve herself did not recall the song after she sung it that night. She started rocking after singing the song and later, turned to Dr. Lord before uttering the following words, "Some songs, like some visions, are a mystery only God knows about. These songs are like important questions I have pondered over the years. No one has the answer to those questions. That is, no one but God. Yet we search for the answer to the questions but resist going to the keeper of the answers." Someone might have interpreted her cryptic statement as the ramblings of a mad person—everyone except her therapist. Dr. Lord remained silent while his patient soothed herself by rocking.

Clad in a hospital gown and her hair up in a bun, the normally-sad woman seemed vibrant and peaceful. Perhaps because the room conjured positive memories of her childhood, or maybe she could finally see with clarity. "I miss sitting on the old rocking chair with my mother. It has been a very long time since I have seen her." Eve reminisced about her relationship with her mom as she allowed the tears to flow freely down her face. "She was a great woman, kind, humble, and always thinking about others."

"You seem to have a lot of respect for your mother," Dr. Lord interjected.

"Yes, she had her faults though," Eve responded with a hint of sadness in her voice. "I respect her but at the same time, I am angry with her."

"Why are you angry?" Dr. Lord asked, but he already knew the answer. "It is interesting that you speak about your mom as if she is gone but also as if she is still alive."

"What do you make of that?" Eve did not realize that she spoke about her mom both in the past tense and the present tense.

Dr. Lord revisited Eve's previous statement about her mom. "Would you like to talk about your anger toward your mother?" he asked.

"Mom chose to look the other way sometimes. She was strong but fearful, burying her head in the sand when faced with ugliness," Eve responded.

"What do you mean by ugliness?" Eve got quiet for a second as she thought about her response. "Some family secrets are too ugly to talk about. I guess my mom felt that our family secret was too ugly to deal with." Eve did not sound like a mentally ill person; she sounded lucid at this point. It was hard sometimes to distinguish between Eve's reality and fantasy.

Suddenly Eve got up from the rocking chair and walked over to the dresser next to a small window on the other side of the room. "I don't recall this window being here," she said, looking puzzled. "I would have remembered having an escape route."

Dr. Lord took a mental note of her description of the window but allowed his patient to talk and explore the room. "I remember this." It was a small jewelry box her dad gave her for her sixteenth birthday. She opened the door of the wardrobe-shaped jewelry box and took out a shiny object. "This is my mother's necklace. She gave it to me when I was a teenager." Eve looked at the tiny cross on a delicate gold chain. "I wore this every day. I don't remember ever taking it off." Dr. Lord watched as Eve unpacked the joy and pain of her childhood. "I promised her I would not take it off because she got it from her mother." She turned back and looked at the rocking chair and smiled. "Sometimes I imagine my grandmother rocking my mom on the same chair she rocked me while recounting the same Bible stories." Suddenly her facial expression changed. She looked concerned. "We didn't talk a lot about Grandma or Grandpa."

"Do you know why your parents didn't talk about them?" Dr. Lord asked, but Eve didn't have a good answer.

The room became silent for at least ten minutes. No one in the room spoke. Eve walked back over to the window and looked outside as if gazing into the past or perhaps the future. "I love my parents. I love both of them. I miss them," Eve said over and over. However, something seemed amiss. Her proclamation of love for her parents appeared to be at odds with her flat affect. It was apparent Eve struggled to convince Dr. Lord that she loved her parents—perhaps to convince herself.

Dr. Lord took advantage of the moment to take his client on a deeper dive. "Talk about your relationship with your dad. What was he like?" Before Eve was able to answer the question, she experienced a strange sensation. Her body became heavy, and a heavy fog filled the room. "Dr. Lord," Eve cried out, "I feel like I am falling." It was not long after she had the sensation of falling that she heard a faint voice beckoning her to wake up.

"Eve, wake up it's almost 9:00 a.m. Good morning, sleepyhead. Are you ready to have breakfast?" Maria walked in with a breakfast tray and a smile.

Eve stretched and yawned. She did not seem bothered by the wake-up call. "I am hungry; what's for breakfast?"

"Well, let's see. I think you will be happy, Eve. They have your favorite foods," Maria teased her as she peeked under the covered plate. "Surprise! It's your favorite—pancake with crispy bacon and eggs." Eve seemed pleased. She was in a good mood despite having her sleep interrupted by her night visitors as she called them. She had become more peaceful with each significant breakthrough. Perhaps each visitation brought her closer to finding the missing piece.

Eve leisurely ate her breakfast before taking a shower and finishing her morning routine. She looked forward to her appointment with Dr. Lord. She hummed as she combed her hair and applied some makeup. "I need to remind Maria to take me to my appointment," Eve told herself as she walked toward the nurse's station, anticipating her meeting with her doctor. The staff was surprised to see her approach the station to get Maria. Normally Maria or one of the other nurses would have to remind Eve about her appointment; the staff often coaxed her to see Dr. Lord.

"The last couple of sessions with Dr. Lord must have been very productive. Eve seemed eager to journey back to the seventh floor," Maria commented to another nurse at the station when she saw Eve approach the nurses' station.

"Hi, Maria, are you ready to take me to my appointment?" Eve asked with expectancy.

"Give me ten minutes." Maria reminded Eve that she had other patients to take care of before escorting her to the seventh floor. "I will take you to your appointment as soon as I am finished taking Ms. Johnson's blood pressure."

"Okay," Eve responded before going back to the room.

As promised, Maria knocked on Eve's door, ready to take her to the seventh floor. "Hold on, I am coming." Eve hurried out to catch up with Maria who headed toward the elevator. Eve beamed as she talked about her recent breakthrough in therapy, but Maria was all business. The elevator ride was quick.

"Here we are," Maria announced as the elevator stopped on the seventh floor.

"Hello, Dr. Lord," Eve greeted the doctor who was standing in the lobby, talking to his receptionist.

"Hello, Eve, I will be ready to see you in two minutes. Let me finish up my notes."

"Sure, Dr. Lord. I will sit in the waiting room." Eve turned toward the nurse and reassured her that she would be fine sitting in the lobby alone. "Maria, you don't have to wait with me. I will be okay." Eve seemed to be in control of her emotions; in fact, she seemed to be in control of her life.

"Are you sure?" Maria asked, surprised by Eve's sudden sense of independence. "I will pick you up after your session," Maria said, pleasantly surprised by Eve's upbeat attitude.

For the first time since being admitted to the psychiatric ward, Eve walked in to Dr. Lord's office ready to discuss the pain that kept her silent for many years. She felt safe to talk about the secret that made her feel shame and kept her in isolation. Eve was ready to trust someone with her pain, ready to break free from the tomb that kept her from experiencing life.

Dr. Lord started by exchanging pleasantries. Although he had a feeling Eve was ready to address some of the painful issues in her life, he did not want to press her. "How has your day been so far?"

Eve ignored the pleasantries and dove right into the session. "I loved my father but felt confused by the type of love he showed me." Dr. Lord looked at her with compassion but allowed her to continue sharing. "My mom was loving, and I know she loved me. I think that she was a fearful woman." Eve rehashed the last session but did not give Dr. Lord an opportunity to interrupt with questions. "My mom turned a blind eye to the pain we experienced as a family. Maybe she saw it but was unable to do anything about it. We lived in isolation, trying to keep our secrets inside, but it kept others from coming in. No one was able to rescue me—they could not see inside the tomb." Dr. Lord allowed her to tell the story without interrupting.

"My life started out so good—great parents. I felt supported and safe—like a princess in a castle surrounded by guards. I often wondered if the guards were aware that they needed to protect me from the danger inside the castle. I feel bad for my mother, she did not live the life she could." Eve's memories brought pain but also elicited joy.

Dr. Lord finally interrupted with a question about her last comment. "What do you mean when you say your mom did not live the life she could?" Dr. Lord purposefully chose not to address Eve's veiled attempt to talk about what may have happened at the hands of her father, at least not yet.

Eve pondered Dr. Lord's question before responding. She seemed tentative about her readiness to talk about her family. "I think my mom had the skills and ability to have a great career. I understand that women in those days were expected to be great mothers and wives. They weren't supposed to think about their vocation. I wonder why she did not leave my dad and create a great life for the both of us. She had to know what he was doing."

At this junction, many therapists inquire about the obvious concerns about her father. Dr. Lord chose not to address it. Instead he focused on the anger toward her parents and the need for forgiveness.

Eve continued recounting her story; this time, she did so from a first-person standpoint. Eve never really said what happened; she danced around the subject. "Did you know that I wanted to be a therapist? I actually went to school for a little while to get my graduate degree but never finished. I often pretended to have my own practice. I helped many people. I think I would have been a good therapist." It was difficult to know how much of her story was real.

Dr. Lord interjected. "I heard you say that you did not finish school. How did you help people in therapy if you were not really a therapist?" Eve did not respond to the question.

Dr. Lord looked at his patient with compassion, sensing she may have experienced something traumatic. "Did you ever wonder who would help you?" Eve placed her hand over her mouth as if surprised by the question.

She took a few seconds before answering. "I always felt there was someone who was trying to guide me out of my despair. You know, lift me out of the tomb. I felt a presence, but I did not understand it."

"Do you feel that presence now?" Dr. Lord inquired.

"Each time I have one of my dreams, I feel as if that presence guides me to the answer to my questions," Eve directly responded to the question but chose not to elaborate further.

Instead Eve redirected the conversation by asking an unrelated question. "Do you think I am a bad person?"

"Why do you ask that question?" Dr. Lord inquired.

"They say I did something bad to my parents. I don't remember what happened or why I am here. I only remember meeting you. Everything else seem like a blur. It feels like nothing outside of this room matters. Nothing else seem real!" Eve's confusion mounted. She seemed to fade into the background like a watermark. Dr. Lord watched as his patient's persona disappeared from the room. Just like the watermark on a page, Eve slowly faded. Strange! Dr. Lord did not seem concerned, but Eve appeared worried. "What's happening?" she questioned the strange sensation that overtook her, but Dr. Lord reassured her that it was part of the journey.

"I must say, this session is unlike any other since I was hospitalized. I feel like I have reached a new height both emotionally and spiritually."

"How so?" Dr. Lord asked.

"Well, I have become more dependent on you but independent at the same time."

"Interesting, tell me more." Dr. Lord encouraged her to express her feelings about the process.

"I think I am learning to trust you and depend on my instincts to deal with the pain that brought me here. In fact, I have learned to trust others like Maria, Angel, and even Hope."

"How does it feel to put your trust in others?" Dr. Lord inquired.

"I have never been able to trust anyone besides Mom and Dad," Eve responded.

"Why is that?"

"I spent most of my time with them, plus I didn't..." Her voice trailed.

"You didn't what?" Dr. Lord asked.

"Dr. Lord, I am not sure how to say this."

"What do you want to say?" Dr. Lord tried to encourage his patient to release the secret that had become a stronghold in her life.

However, Eve began feeling an unexpected sensation that took her focus from the session. "What is happening to me? I don't understand." Eve became afraid and held on tightly to her chair. "I feel dizzy." She was unable to explain the bizarre sensation and looked to Dr. Lord for comfort.

"Don't be afraid, take a deep breath." Dr. Lord reassured her. "I want you to count backward from ten. Ten, nine, eight, seven..."

"Ms. Di Angelo, can you hear me?"

"She is not responding, doctor. Do you think she is going to be okay?" The young nurse seemed concerned but hopeful that the emergency-room doctor had everything under control.

"Her vitals are normal. I think she is going to be okay." Dr. Browne reassured the nurse.

Eve slowly opened her eyes and saw a group of nurses and doctors standing around. She struggled to speak through the oxygen mask that helped her with her breathing. "Where... am...I?" Barely audible, she spoke in a raspy voice.

"You are in the hospital, don't you remember what happened?" one of the nurses responded to Eve as other hospital personnel scurried around, taking care of other patients. "Welcome back. You have been unconscious for a couple of hours. You arrived with smoke inhalation following a fire at the apartment.

"Where are my parents? I want to see Dr. Lord. Where is Maria?"

Confused by Eve's babblings, the nurse tried to reassure her. "Ms. Di Angelo, there is no Dr. Lord at this hospital."

"What do you mean there is no Dr. Lord here? He has been helping me for a while."

"Let's get your blood pressure checked, and someone will be in shortly to answer your questions," the nurse reassured a confused and scared Eve.

The nurse ran to get the doctor who had stepped out of the room. "Dr. Browne, I don't think the patient remembers what happened. She is asking about her parents and a Dr. Lord. She is obviously confused. What should we say?"

Dr. Browne looked at his notes and asked the nurse to administer a sedative to calm the patient down. "She is obviously hallucinating, or perhaps her brain created a protective story to shield her from the trauma she experienced. It is not unusual for a victim of trauma who also has been unconscious to confabulate."

Confused, the nurse asked the doctor to explain the word. "*Confabulate* is a term used in psychiatry to indicate that someone has fabricated an imaginary experience to compensate for memory loss. I am not a psychiatrist, but it sure seems like that is what this patient is doing."

"I hope she gets to the bottom of what happened and is able to heal." Rhonda (the nurse) and Dr. Browne walked out the room and turned out the light so their new patient could rest.

Part 4

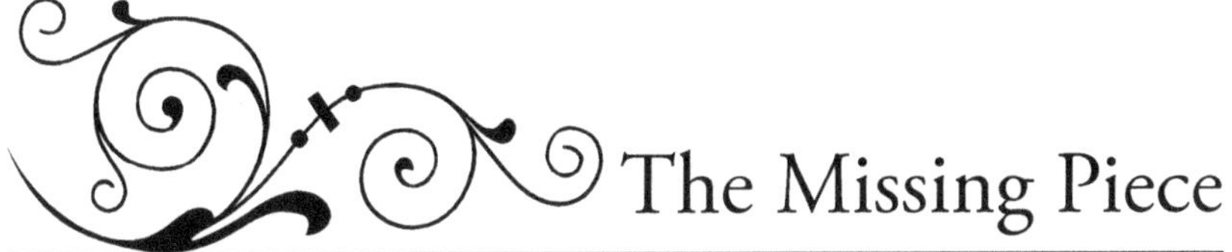

The Missing Piece

From the time a person enters this world until the day he/she leaves the earth, they search for the missing piece. The last piece of the puzzle, you know, the part that makes the person complete. We see ourselves as a puzzle undone, and we go on a quest to find completion. The missing piece of the puzzle manifests in many ways: emotional, spiritual, physical completion. We exercise to lose weight, build muscles, or change our appearance. We read books and other materials in hopes that we may gain knowledge and wisdom. We seek help from therapists and spiritual advisors in an effort to gain a better understanding of self. We look for the missing piece in others—romantic relationships, platonic relationships, even virtual relationships become the focus of those searching for the missing piece of the puzzle. In the final analysis, we struggle to understand who we are, why we are here, and determine our purpose.

"The baby is coming. I see the head."

It was early Thursday morning in September when the maternity ward at Bellevue hospital was awakened by the announcement of a new life. "What a beautiful child." The charge nurse and all the other nurses on the ward could not stop gushing about the beauty of the baby that graced John and Beverly Di Angelo's lives. The couple beamed at the sight of their firstborn—it was a girl.

"We will call her Eve," they told their OBGYN doctor and the nurses who stood in awe of the child's beauty. She had beautiful gold colored ringlets, full lips, and slanted hazel eyes with olive skin tone.

"You did well, Beverly," her husband said as he stroked her hair.

"Yep, we did well," she responded as she puckered her lips, waiting for him to kiss her.

"I need you to get some rest, honey. You just went through thirteen hours of hard labor. I am going to go home and feed Casper, and I will return first thing in the morning."

"Honey, don't forget to bring my blue dress with the tiny flowers. I want to wear that when I am released from the hospital."

"I won't forget, dear, remember I love the way you look in that dress." John kissed his wife on the forehead before kissing his new daughter who was lying in the basinet next to her mother's hospital bed. "See you tomorrow."

"Okay," Beverly responded with a smile.

John and Beverly were an average couple in their early thirties. Both worked to afford their two-bedroom, two-bath apartment in Manhattan. Beverly grew up in New Jersey but moved to New York after college where she met John. Both attended out-of-town colleges but returned to be near family. John wasn't very close to his family, but Beverly was. They adored their little girl and gave her everything parents thought their child needed to have success in the world.

The one thing she was missing was a sense of identity.

Beverly was a pretty five-foot-two-inch woman of mixed race. No one ever knew what she was mixed with because her biological parents died when she was young, and she was adopted by an older couple. She often wondered who her biological parents were. Did they love her? How did they die? Her adoptive parents kept that information from her. They didn't talk about her biological parents. Now they were also gone. She was alone in the world, of course, beside her husband and her beautiful baby girl.

John, on the other hand, was a tall, muscular, blond man who prided himself in the way he looked. He was not close to his family. Once he left for college, he did not keep in touch with them. John had a turbulent childhood, but he did not talk about it. The contrast between husband and wife was stark. Beverly was simple and quiet while John was more boisterous and intimidating. Beverly had parents who were supportive and present while John's parents were loud and not as supportive. It was hard to determine what brought these two together. They say opposites attract, but those same differences often pull people apart.

Beverly cut down her hours when she got pregnant. She only worked part-time, but she made enough money as a bookkeeper to help John with the expenses. She loved her job, and it gave her a sense of purpose, but she was a new mom now. Although her part-time status afforded her the opportunity to stay home with their new bundle of joy, she struggled with the thought of leaving Eve with a stranger. Babysitters and work were the last thing on Beverly's mind today. She could only think about the beautiful baby in her arms. "You are my sunshine, the reason I exist now." The new mom looked into baby's eyes as she promised to keep her safe and love her.

Beverly allowed her thoughts to wander briefly to the new nursery she fixed up before going into the hospital, but she could not take her eyes off her child. "Eve, you are going to love your room. Mommy and Daddy got you stuffed animals, a beautiful old-fashioned crib, and a rocking chair next to the door. I am going to rock you while I read stories just like my mom did." The rocking chair was a family heirloom she cherished. She remembered sitting on her adoptive mom's lap at the age of five, rocking while she listened to Bible stories about great people who overcame adversities. She always dreamed of the day she would sit on the same chair and rock her own child—finally she would have that chance. She imagined reading nursery rhymes and stories that would delight and fascinate her baby girl.

Beverly recalled her favorite childhood story was about Jonah in the belly of the whale. She remembers her mom starting the story by saying, "Jonah tried to hide from God because he did not want to obey, and he was swallowed by a big fish. We need to be obedient if we don't want to be swallowed by a fish." She and her mom would laugh and make fish faces, and then her mom would tell the rest of the story. "God called Jonah to preach to Nineveh, a land far away. Jonah hated the idea because the people from Nineveh were Israel's greatest enemies, so he tried to run in the opposite direction. Jonah took a boat to a place named Tarsish in order to hide from God and what he told him to do. Unfortunately a big storm tossed the boat, and everyone got scared. They blamed Jonah for the storm and tossed him overboard."

"What happened after that, Mom?" Beverly questioned her mom. She always had a big smile on her face. "How did he get there, Mama?" she repeatedly asked in her high-pitched voice. Mom would recount the story over and over. Beverly never got tired of hearing that story. "Great memories, I miss my mom and dad," she said to herself as she got her bundle of joy ready to go home. Beverly took one last look at the hospital room before gently lifting Eve out of the basinet next to her hospital bed. "So long, room. I won't miss you because we are going to our home."

"Welcome home," the big banner hanging on the living room wall welcomed both Beverly and little Eve to the tiny apartment. Little pink flowers adorned the banner, and a vase filled with red flowers sat conspicuously on the dining room table. John walked into the apartment first to make sure everything was just right for his two favorite girls.

Beaming with pride and excitement, he pulled out a small stuffed animal from behind his back. "This is for Eve, and those red roses are for you."

"John, you shouldn't have. I didn't want you to spend money, honey. We are going to have a lot of expenses."

"I just want to spoil our little girl," he responded while planting a kiss on her cheek. "I will never forget this day." It was a sunny day, not a cloud in the sky. The sunlight entered the tiny apartment through a picture window (the only window facing the street). The gold rays kissed baby Eve's ringlet, creating a halo-like effect over her head. John pulled out an old camera and took a picture of mom and daughter. The picture hung in the living room through the years.

ଔ

"Where did the time go?" Beverly asked as she and John sang Happy Birthday to their not-so-little baby girl. It was Eve's first birthday. The picture on the wall with Beverly cradling little Eve reminded them that time had passed since the birth of their little girl. Both parents stood over their daughter as she put her hand in the cake and smeared it all over her face, trying to eat it. "Today we celebrate your first birthday with cake and ice cream."

"Honey, you make us so happy. We don't know what we would do if you were not in our lives."

John chimed in, "I agree, you are my number 1. You were my number one, Beverly, but Eve stole my heart."

"I understand, honey, she has that effect on everyone," Beverly said jokingly but a little jealous that she was no longer his favorite girl.

"We will not let you out of the house until you are thirty." John said to his little girl before turning to his wife. "In fact, I will not allow her to date until she is thirty-five."

"Honey, she will have to get married some time," Beverly protested while shaking her head.

The couple and their little girl lived a very happy life. The outside world did not seem to affect the Di Angelo family. John continued to work while Beverly cared for Eve and worked less than twenty hours per week. Beverly intended to go back to work full-time when Eve was old enough to attend school—she never did. They imagined sending Eve to a private school where she would be prepared to attend college. Perhaps she would become a lawyer or doctor.

The Di Angelo family went about their daily routine while the years went by almost unnoticed. Beverly submerged herself in her mommy duties while holding down her part-time job at the accounting firm. John continued being the primary breadwinner. He took care of the family's financial needs. Eve, well, she grew into a beautiful young woman who loved her parents and enjoyed the safe place they created for her.

"Mom, where are you?"

"I'm here, honey, what's the emergency?"

"My first day of junior high school was fantastic. I can't wait to tell you all about my day." Behind the façade of some happy families lay dormant, bitter secrets that threaten to dismantle the walls that keep secrets in and others out. The Di Angelo family looked like the picture-perfect family—the loving, hardworking husband, the nurturing wife, and perfect daughter.

Eve was elated and could not wait to describe her day in great detail. "Today I met Mary, my best friend." Eve's face lit up as she shared her day with her mother.

"How is she your best friend if you just met her today?"

"I have a feeling that she will be my best friend forever," Eve responded to her mother's sarcastic question.

"That's nice, Eve, I am glad you made friends today."

"Mom, I tell you that junior high school is going to be the best time of my life. I am so glad I am going to that school."

While Eve rambled on about her first day of junior high school, Beverly could not help but to think about Eve's first day of kindergarten. She took out the picture of a precocious child with a couple missing teeth and the biggest smile ever. The curly-haired girl in the picture wore a dress with tiny pink flowers and a sweater with pearl-like buttons. Eve loved to dress up even as child. "I cannot believe how fast time passed. My girl was so little not so long ago," Beverly muttered to herself.

"Mom, are you listening to me?" Eve's voice interrupted Beverly's stroll down memory lane.

"Of course, honey. I was just looking at your picture and thinking that you are growing up too fast." Eve smiled and kept chatting.

"I can't wait for you to meet Mary and her mom." The pair could not be more different. While Mary was a quiet girl, Eve was gregarious and very assertive.

"Mary is so nice, Mom. She sat with me and shared her lunch."

"That's nice, honey," Beverly answered as she stirred the spaghetti sauce on the stove.

Unphased by her mom's apparent lack of interest in the story, Eve continued chatting away. "My teachers are also nice." Eve's short sentences were filled with passion and appeared to be so interesting to her. Beverly, on the other hand, patiently pretended to listen to her daughter without interrupting or even really paying close attention. Just as Beverly thought to herself, *I don't know how much longer I can pretend to be interested in Eve's long story*, she heard John's key in the door.

"Hi, honey, welcome home. How was your day?"

"Tired!" John was visibly exhausted from his construction job. He started working construction after he was unable to get a job in his field of study.

"Hi, Daddy, how are you?" Bubbling with excitement, Eve jumped up to give her father a hug. Eve continued to have a close relationship with her parents especially her father.

"Hi, princess, how was your day?" Beverly gave John a look that said, "You don't want to know." She did not verbalize what she was thinking, but John got the picture. "Maybe you can tell me all about it after dinner."

"Okay, Dad. You are going to be so surprised when I tell you what happened today at school."

"I bet I will be princess." The couple treated their daughter as if she was a little girl and not a teenager. Eve acted younger than she was. While other teen girls were interested in boys, she seemed interested in daydreaming and storytelling.

After dinner, Beverly washed the dishes and cleaned up the kitchen before sitting in the living room with John and their daughter. John's mind seemed a million miles away as Eve shared the story about meeting her new best friend. Recognizing something might be wrong with John, Beverly asked Eve to prepare for bed. "Why don't you go and take your shower and put on your pajamas after completing your homework?"

"All right, Mom," Eve responded without protesting.

"John, what's going on?" Beverly asked with a worried look on her face.

"Nothing. I'm not in the mood to talk right now." John had been somewhat moody and not very talkative lately. Although Beverly noticed the change in her husband's demeanor, she chose not to escalate the situation.

"Well, John, I won't force you to talk, but I really wish you would. Eventually what is bothering you will affect the family."

John knew he had to talk to his wife sooner or later but decided later might be best. "I am just tired, lots going on at work, and I don't really feel like talking about it."

The couple went to bed without speaking another word about John's mood. As customary for Beverly, she read a couple Bible verses and prayed before turning off the night-light. Neither one slept; John stared at the ceiling while Beverly closed her eyes and continued to pray.

"Dear, Lord, please touch my husband and help him deal with whatever is bothering him. You know I love him, but he won't let me in. What should I do? Please draw him closer to you and make him see how he is affecting his family. Amen." Beverly's short prayer was filled with power. She knew her marriage would be in trouble if she did nothing, so she chose to depend on God for the answer. Beverly couldn't resist giving God one final reminder. "This is out of my hands, God, if you don't fix it, we are in trouble."

The following morning, the couple got up and went about their normal day. "Beverly, have you seen my shoes?"

"They are probably where you left them yesterday—under the bed," Beverly yelled from the kitchen. "You haven't said a word since yesterday, and now you want to talk? I guess I am worth talking to when you need me," Beverly muttered as she slammed pots and pans. She was obviously still upset about John's unwillingness to talk the night before.

John got dressed for work while Beverly prepared breakfast for the family. They ignored each other and pretended everything was okay in front of Eve. As soon as their daughter walked in the kitchen, Beverly and John changed their demeanor.

"Hi, Mom and Dad, did you sleep well?"

"Hi, honey, how are you?" John responded to his daughter with a smile.

"Hi, honey, are you hungry? I was going to make pancakes, but we don't have much time," Beverly chimed in as she poured cereal in a bowl. "How much milk do you want? Say when."

"When." Eve responded in a childlike manner, seemingly oblivious to the tense climate in the room.

Although Eve was thirteen at this point, she seemed emotionally younger than her peers. Eve was naïve and seldom paid attention to her surroundings. "Who is taking me to school today?" Eve asked, looking at both parents. Perhaps she was more aware of the tension than her parents gave her credit for but chose not to say anything.

"What's wrong with taking the school bus?" Beverly asked, wondering if something was wrong.

"Nothing is wrong, Mom. I just thought I could spend some extra time with you or Dad." Sometimes children are more perceptive than parents give them credit. Her parents tried to protect her from every negative emotion but unwittingly hampered her emotional growth.

Eve's emotional stagnation was quite evident. She did not seem interested in boys like other girls her age; she did not even seem eager to hang out after school with her best friend. Eve was content being with Mom and Dad especially hanging out with her dad. She relished the safety and security her family provided and didn't seem to need anyone else.

"I will take you to school," John spoke up as he held his arms open to give his daughter a hug.

Excited that she did not have to take the bus, Eve talked incessantly during the drive to school as her father quietly listened. "Dad, are you hearing what I am saying?"

"Yes, honey, I am listening to you, but Daddy has a lot on his mind right now."

"Really!" Eve exclaimed, surprised that her father could have anything but her on his mind. "What's wrong?"

"Don't you worry your pretty little head," John said, mimicking the way cowboys talk. He had not used that make-believe cowboy accent since Eve was a little girl when he pretended to save the little damsel in distress. The exchange did not seem strange to Eve; she loved being treated like a little princess. Her dad's disclosure did not deter Eve from carrying on her previous conversation. Without skipping a beat, she continued telling her story about the latest happenings at school.

Perhaps in an attempt to get Eve to be quiet for a second, John reached out and laid his hands on her lap. He then reached over and kissed her lightly on the forehead. "You know I love you, don't you?"

Eve looked at her dad for a second before responding; "Of course you love me, Daddy." She found the interaction a bit strange but did not want to make a big deal. "So, Dad, what are we going to do when you get home from work. You know, I would love to go to the mall and get a new outfit." Eve continued talking for a few more minutes before she finally stopped and stared out the window.

John barely looked at his daughter after the awkward exchange. He simply reminded her that he would get her from school. "I will pick you up after school today."

"Really, why, Dad?" Eve asked, curious about the reason for her dad wanting to pick her up. John never picked her up from school before. Generally Eve took the school bus; however, from time to time, Beverly picked up her daughter from school to have a special day together.

"Wouldn't it be fun to go and have a bite to eat with your ol' dad for a change?"

"Sure, Dad, that would be awesome."

"Well, it's a date. Here we are, honey. Don't forget to meet me in front of the school."

"Okay, Dad. I won't forget."

Eve jumped out of the car and said goodbye to her dad before running off to catch up with one of her friends. John sat in the car for a minute, watching his daughter before driving away. Although it was a sunny and clear day, there seemed to be a dark cloud over the car; perhaps it only covered John's mind. Fraught by the stress of losing his job, he took a minute in the car to gather his thoughts. "What am I going to do all day?" John asked himself before deciding to spend the day in the park reading the newspaper.

Back in the apartment, Beverly spent the day cleaning and washing clothes, unaware of the dark cloud that would soon roll into their lives and affect their happiness. She hummed familiar hymns and old songs to keep herself entertained and distracted from the monotony of her chores. Unfortunately the hymns could not keep her mind from wandering back to the exchange she had with John the night before. Beverly knew something was wrong; in fact, the couple had been distant for several months.

The phone rang, giving Beverly a much-needed break. "Hello, this is Beverly, who is calling?" The voice on the other end was her good friend Bertha. "Hey, Bertha, I have not heard from you in many moons. How are you? It is certainly good to hear from you. How are the kids?"

"John and Eve are doing okay. In fact, John took Eve to school today because he did not have to be at work until later." After a long pause, Bertha said she may have seen John downtown today. "You might be mistaken because he went back to work after dropping Eve off at school." The way Beverly responded signaled her discomfort with the conversation. Bertha must have picked up on Beverly's discomfort because the conversation quickly changed to a safer topic. The friends began talking about their children, recipes, and the latest workplace gossip.

"We should take your kids to the park next week." Beverly proposed, an obvious attempt to avoid revisiting the conversation about John. "There is a new park a couple of blocks from my house that also has a dog park. Maybe Eve and I can take Casper for a walk while your children play on the swings." It was obvious the discussion began to run its course because the pauses got longer as Beverly and Bertha seem to run out of things to say. "I will talk with you later, Bertha. I am so glad you called."

Bertha worked as a receptionist at the firm where Beverly did bookkeeping part-time. The two became fast friends because of their strong Christian belief and quiet demeanor. Bertha was tall with dark hair and glasses. She was a very unassuming person who blended in to the point of almost becoming invisible. She had been working at the firm for at least two years before Beverly was hired. Bertha did not have a college degree, but she was very smart. In fact, she hoped to own a business one day. Unfortunately her lack of self-esteem seemed to get in the way of her goals; she always stopped short of achieving her dreams.

Beverly on the other hand believed she could do anything. Perhaps she would have if she had not gotten married and had a child. Her old-fashioned thinking hindered her from stepping out of her comfort zone. She often daydreamed of going back to school to become a therapist or social worker. She enjoyed helping others especially other women. She shared her dreams with Bertha who often encouraged her to go back to school to complete her degree. Beverly knew she was smart and did not doubt that she would succeed if she went back to school but felt conflicted about juggling a family and work. Like many women of her era, Beverly felt that it was important to give up her career to take care of her husband and children.

Since marrying John, Beverly's world became tethered to the apartment. She seldom did anything outside of the home besides attending work and church. Once in a while, she went to lunch with Bertha or spoke on the phone. Bertha's children were a little younger than Eve and required more of her attention, further limiting the friends' ability to connect. Although Eve was a teenager and could take care of herself, Beverly felt apprehensive about leaving her home alone. This meant that Beverly seldom went out with friends or have a date night with John. Her husband and daughter become her entire world while church and work were the occasional break from the cocoon the couple created to shield them from the world.

Beverly had barely hung up the phone after talking to Bertha when the phone rang again. This time, it was John. "Hi, honey, where are you?"

"I am going to pick up Eve and take her to have some ice cream."

"That's nice but just one scoop. I don't want her to ruin her dinner by eating ice cream." Although Eve was bothered by John's decision to take their daughter for ice cream right before dinner, she chose not to address the issue.

"Do you need something while I am out?" John asked in an upbeat tone. He was in a better mood than he was earlier at breakfast.

"No, I think I have everything under control. Don't forget dinner is at 6:00 p.m. Hurry home. I hear Eve in the background. Let her know that I love her."

"Okay, honey." John hurried Beverly off the phone.

"Hi, Daddy." Eve ran to give her father a hug.

"Are you ready for a surprise?" John asked with a sheepish smile on his face. Eve could hardly contain her excitement.

"Where are we going?"

"We are going to the ice creamery to get your favorite ice-cream cone."

"Vanilla with chocolate syrup?" Eve said, licking her lips.

"Get in the car and let's get there before all the ice scream is gone." John still treated his daughter like she was ten years old, and she did not seem to mind.

"How was your day, Daddy?" Eve asked as she licked the melting ice cream off her hands.

"I had a good day. I ran a few errands and drove to a friend's house to talk."

"I thought you had to work?"

"Don't tell your mom, she will get mad if she knew." For the first time, John asked his daughter to cover for him. Eve was a little surprised but agreed to keep the secret from her mother. "I don't want your mom to worry about me."

"Okay, Daddy, don't worry. I won't say a word." Little did Eve know this would be the first of many secrets she would be asked to keep from her mother.

John saw the concern on his daughter's face and wanted to reassure her. "Don't worry, Eve, let's just focus on having a great day eating ice cream."

Both father and daughter seemed to enjoy the time they spent together which made it difficult to let Eve know that it was almost time to go home. "Ready to go?" John prepared his daughter to leave the ice cream parlor. "I am not ready to go, but I know Mom will be worried."

John reached over and kissed his daughter. "You are such a caring child." Eve smiled and walked ahead of her dad.

The ride home got a little awkward when John placed his hand on his daughter's leg and reminded her how much he loved her. The touch would not have been awkward if it did not linger so long. Both John and Beverly were demonstrative parents and freely showed affection, but this touch felt a little different. Eve turned her head and looked out the window at the scenery as they drove on the highway. She remained silent the rest of the ride and kept her eyes on the road.

It wasn't long before they got home. The ice scream parlor was not far from the apartment building. "Hi, honey, we are home." John walked into the kitchen where Beverly sat at the kitchen table, reading her Bible. Eve trailed behind her dad, not saying much.

"Hi, how was the father/daughter ice-cream date?"

Eve's demeanor immediately changed. "We had so much fun. Daddy let me get my favorite ice-cream cone."

Feeling guilty because he allowed Eve to have ice scream, John chimed in, "She only got a small cone because I did not want her to lose her appetite."

"Thanks, John. Dinner will be ready in a few minutes."

"We had such a good time, Mom. I can't wait for you to go with us next time." Eve wanted to go on about their day, but Beverly was ready to sit down and have family dinner. Eve pretended that everything was okay, although she was concerned about her father's inappropriate touch earlier. She did not want to worry her mom nor add to the stress her parents were experiencing.

"Can I skip dinner tonight? My tummy hurts a little," Eve asked her mom's permission to skip dinner and go to her bedroom.

"John!" Beverly shouted his name, obviously irritated with her husband. She gave him a look that could have burned a hole in him. "You said that she only had a small ice cream cone."

"She did, but I think her stomach is upset because she might have eaten it too fast." Beverly did not believe John's rationale but decided not to cause an argument.

The tension between the couple was palpable, but they tried not to affect their daughter. "Eve, please get your homework done and take your bath to get ready for bed."

"I will, Mom," Eve responded as she looked through her bag for her homework. "Mom, can I call Mary after I am done with my homework and bath?"

"Sure, honey, but I thought you had a stomachache?"

"It's not that bad, I just don't want to eat anything that would make it worse."

Beverly relented and gave her daughter permission to talk on the phone. "You can only talk for fifteen minutes."

"Okay, Mom. I won't stay on the phone very long. I just want to tell Mary what I am wearing tomorrow so we can be twins."

Eve ran to her room to do her homework before calling her friend. John and Beverly went to their bedroom to talk in private. "I am concerned that you are not telling me everything." Beverly started the conversation, hoping to get John to talk.

"I am tired, can we talk tomorrow?" John was dismissive of his wife—a departure from the way he treated her at the beginning of their marriage.

The first few years of their marriage, he was attentive and made her feel like she was the most important person in the world. Recently though, his behavior had changed. John became distant, and Beverly was unable to put her finger on the reason for the change. "John, I don't think we should wait until tomorrow to talk about this." Beverly insisted that the couple have a serious talk about their relationship.

"I told you I don't want to talk." John's voice got louder and meaner.

"Please lower your voice. I don't want to upset Eve."

John walked to the kitchen and got a beer out of the refrigerator before sitting on the couch in the living room. He clearly did not want to address Beverly's question. Perhaps he feared where the conversation might lead.

Beverly relented and went to bed. She did not immediately go to sleep. She lay staring at the ceiling, wondering what she could do to get her husband to open up. A million thoughts ran through her mind as she tried to answer the looming question in her head: *Why doesn't he want to talk to me*? She tormented herself with question after question for which she had no answer. Exhausted, Beverly finally fell asleep.

In the meantime, John sat in the living room and drank one beer after another while he watched TV. After a few beers and feeling a little drunk, he decided it was time to go to sleep. John could barely walk; completely inebriated, he stumbled into Eve's bedroom to check on her before going to bed. John slowly opened her door and peeked his head in the room and caught a glance of his sleeping daughter. Curled up in a fetal position, Eve slept like a baby. She reminded him of the little princess he escorted to her kindergarten class not long ago. She was so dependent on him which made John feel needed. "Look at my baby. She is growing up. I wish time would slow down"

As he stood outside the door, staring at his daughter and thinking about how fast she was growing, something came over him. John walked in the room to give her a goodnight kiss on the forehead. Instead he allowed his hand to slightly rub her leg. He immediately moved his hand and walked out the room. "What am I thinking?" John asked himself as he walked to his room. "I am glad she did not wake up," he mumbled as he walked out of the room. He did not notice that Eve opened her eyes after he turned around to walk out the room. She pulled the covers over her head and pretended to go back to sleep.

John went back to his bedroom and lay next to his wife but did not touch her. The couple always cuddled with each other as they slept, but that seemed to change in the last few months. Although he was a little drunk, John was aware of his actions and could not stop thinking about it. He got out the bed a couple of times to go to the bathroom. Confused and angry, the flood of thoughts kept him from going back to sleep. John ruminated about what transpired earlier, trying to come up with an explanation or perhaps an excuse. Racked by guilt, he got out of bed and went to the living room to sleep on the couch.

The following morning, Eve and Beverly got up and went about their morning routine. John, on the other hand, was still sleeping. "Good morning, sleepyhead," Beverly greeted her husband even though she was upset because he refused to talk about her concerns regarding his gradual distancing from her. "Did you fall asleep on the couch? Why didn't you come into the bedroom?"

Beverly's line of questioning annoyed John, but he tried not to show it. "I guess I had too many beers and was unable to get up and find my way to the bedroom."

Always the optimist and one who sees the best in everyone, Beverly tried to comfort her husband. "You should have called me, I would have helped you to the bedroom." John tried to change the conversation by talking about what he was going to do in the next few hours.

Saved by the bell! Immediately after the exchange between her parents, Eve walked into the living room. "Good morning, Mom. Good morning, Dad. Did you sleep well last night?"

Both parents simultaneously turned and greeted their daughter. "Hello, honey," both said in unison.

"You guys are twins," Eve said jokingly.

EVE. What's for breakfast, Mom?
BEVERLY. Whatever you want. Today you are making your own breakfast.
EVE. I guess I am having cereal.
BEVERLY. I guess so.

The exchange ended when John said that he would pick Eve up from school again.

"Why are you picking her up? Don't you have to go to work?"

"I have a light day today and just felt it would be good to spend some time with my daughter. I have been extremely busy in the past and did not spend enough time with Eve. She is growing up very fast, and I don't want to miss more precious time with her."

"What is going on? Are you okay? You are scaring me because you normally don't take time off." Beverly thought maybe her husband was having health problems he did not want to talk about.

"Nothing is wrong, I just want to spend more time with my daughter."

"Grab your school bag, Eve. It's time to go."

"Bye, Mom. I will see you after school. I love you." Beverly was left with a pit in her stomach. She did not understand why she felt uneasy. Perhaps she feared losing her husband's affection, or maybe she felt that she was losing her daughter. She refused to think about the alternative. Perhaps John had a terminal illness and did not want to burden the family. Beverly told herself that her thoughts were silly; none of those thoughts were real.

John was not sick, and he loved Eve just as much as she did. In fact, she had more time in the past with Eve because she was a stay-at-home mom for the first few years after giving birth. It was John's time to enjoy their daughter. Perhaps she was being silly and selfish. "Bye, honey, have a nice day. I love you very much and don't you forget that." John kissed Beverly on the cheek and walked out the door with Eve.

Beverly started tidying up the kitchen after her husband and daughter left. She hummed as she cleaned. Anyone observing Beverly would think everything was okay in her world—a PTA mom who took good care of her family. "I can't believe how dusty this apartment gets. Oh, John, you left your jacket on the chair again." Beverly continued to work and talk to herself. Suddenly and without warning, tears started flowing down her cheeks like someone turned on a faucet. Beverly did not know what exactly triggered the tears, but she knew something was wrong. She started feeling dizzy and unable to stand. Overwhelmed by emotions, she sat at the kitchen table and wept bitterly.

It seemed as if several hours had passed before Beverly picked her head up from the table and looked around the kitchen. "I need to get dinner started," She told herself as she wiped her tears and walked over to the stove. The phone rang just as she opened the refrigerator to get the cheese and milk to fix her scallop potatoes. "Hello, who is this?" The person on the other line was her friend Bertha. "Hi, Bertha, how are you? Twice in a row, this is a miracle. You have never called this often before," Beverly said sarcastically. "To what do I owe this pleasure?" Both friends laughed out loud before moving on to the office gossip. Although Beverly was not one for gossiping, it was a welcome relief from dealing with her problems.

It was clear Bertha asked what Beverly was doing because of her response. "I am getting ready to cook. I have been cleaning and got distracted, so I am running a little behind. What are you doing?" The pleasantries were short-lived. It soon became apparent that Bertha was not calling to catch up on office gossip.

"How are you and John doing?" Bertha quickly went to the heart of the matter.

"What do you mean? We are doing well," Beverly responded, irritated by the question. "I think I hear the doorbell." A signal to Bertha that the conversation was over. "I will have to call you back another day." Beverly hung up the phone and burst into tears. "Does everyone know my business?" She asked herself, shaking with fury. Beverly was a private person and did not appreciate anyone prying in her personal life.

The conversation with Bertha struck a cord and caused Beverly to question her relationship with her husband. "What's taking John so long?" Beverly asked herself as she paced back and forth in the kitchen. She looked at the clock several times, becoming even more impatient. "Eve got out of school an hour ago. I hope John did not get distracted and forget to pick her up. What if something happened? What if they got in an accident?" She took a deep breath and reassured herself that John was a responsible parent, and nothing bad happened. "Everything will be okay."

Beverly said a quick prayer and resumed cooking. However, she was unable to shake the thought that something was going on with John. Bertha's question resonated over and over in her mind—how are you and John doing? Finally the question hit Beverly like an arrow through the heart. "I have to get to the bottom of the problem." The couple had been going through what Beverly thought was a rough patch—nothing major. "Don't let your mind play tricks on you, Beverly." She told herself again and again in an attempt to reduce her anxiety.

"Thank God," Beverly exclaimed, followed by a deep breath. She heard John's key in the door and figured she could finally address the issue.

"Hi, Mom, what's for dinner?" Eve greeted her mom in a high-pitched voice.

"Are you hungry?"

"Yes, I am starving."

"How about you, John?"

"Not really." John response was short and measured, fueling Beverly's concerns.

John was very quiet during dinner despite Beverly's attempt to engage him in conversation. Unfortunately he resisted every attempt to connect intimately and emotionally with his wife. *Perhaps Bertha was right*; Beverly thought to herself. *Something was going on with John, and it did not appear to be a passing issue*. "John, can we talk after dinner?"

"Sure, what do you want to talk about?" John said in a very unpleasant tone.

Beverly looked over at her daughter who was enjoying her meal and decided to wait until they were alone. "We can talk later tonight," she said reluctantly.

"Sure." Beverly was becoming used to John's one word or one-sentence responses; however, she vowed to no longer put up with his nasty attitude toward her. She loved her family but felt unloved and unwanted by her husband.

Beverly turned to her daughter. "Eve, do you have homework?"

"I did my homework at school. Maria and I decided to start working on our homework while I waited for Dad to pick me up."

"Let's see what you have." Beverly trusted her daughter but wanted to ensure that her homework was done correctly. Eve skipped past her parents and went to her room to get her workbook. "How was school today?" Beverly asked, feeling a little disconnected from her family.

"It was good." It was obvious Beverly would have to ask probing questions to get a conversation going. Perhaps her daughter's lack of interest in long conversations with her parents was related to the fact that she was a teenager. Beverly wanted a better connection with Eve but was not overly worried that her daughter no longer confided in her. She did not see any danger signs that indicated something was horribly wrong.

"What did you do?"

Eve gave a typical teenage answer. "I don't remember. I just went to my class and then lunch."

Beverly missed the bond she once shared with her daughter. Although she understood that Eve was becoming a young woman, she longed for the closeness they had when her little girl depended on her. "I remember when you couldn't wait to tell me about your day. What happened?"

"Hormones!" John chimed in from the kitchen." The interaction between mom and daughter had become a little distant in recent months. It would not have been so bad if Beverly and John were getting along. The marital discord exacerbated her feelings of loneliness and loss.

She couldn't help but think about the closeness between John and Eve while a chasm separated her from both of them. *What happened? When did this separation begin?* She asked herself but could not put her finger on a specific time or event. *I need to have some alone time with John to talk about our problems.* Beverly decided to create some alone time with her husband. "Would you like to go and spend the weekend with your friend Maria or another classmate?" Beverly tried to get her teenage daughter out of the house for a day or two.

"I have a lot of reading this weekend. I am preparing for a test next week," Eve responded.

"Maybe Maria can come and study with you?" Beverly countered.

"Maybe," Eve said in a very matter-of-fact way. Beverly decided not to push the issue; she would approach her husband after their daughter fell asleep.

Later that night, Beverly unsuccessfully confronted John about the strain in their relationship. "What is going on, John?"

"What do you mean?"

"You know what I mean. We have not talked or been close in a long time. Anytime I try to talk about our problems, you avoid me. You have been picking Eve up from school in an attempt to avoid talking with me or spending time with me." Beverly did not allow John to counter; she interrupted him anytime he tried to say something. It felt as if she was trying to avoid hearing bad news. During a lull, John was finally able to respond, although his answer did not offer clarity nor comfort to his distraught wife.

"I think you should give me some space to figure things out. I don't plan on leaving or getting a divorce, but I need to breathe."

"What do you mean you need to figure things out? How do you think I feel? By the way, why are you talking about divorce?" Beverly yelled, hoping to convey her pain. She wanted John to see how his response to her made her feel. "You have been ignoring and mistreating me."

John remained silent, shocked by the intensity of Beverly's anger. Although the emotionally-charged conversation gave John pause, he refused to tell his wife that he lost his job and felt like his life was spiraling out of control. Beverly continued to talk and cry until she fell asleep from exhaustion.

John was aware that his behavior was causing his wife pain, but his pride got in the way. He waited a few minutes after his wife fell asleep before getting out of the bed to get a glass of cold water. On his way to the kitchen, he peeked in on Eve and saw that she was asleep. *She looks like an angel*, he thought to himself before walking in the room with some trepidation. John stood directly above his daughter and watched her every breath before sitting beside her on the bed. He rubbed her hair and leaned over and kissed her forehead. Eve rolled to the side, facing her dad, and opened her eyes.

"Hi, Dad, what are you doing here?" she asked, confused by his presence in her room.

"Just watching you sleep. You know how much I love you, right?"

"Yes, Dad, I know you love me."

Although Eve felt confused, she was happy for the constant attention she received from her father. The family isolated themselves, leaving their daughter disconnected from outside support or healthy relationships with her peers. "Dad, are you picking me up from school tomorrow?"

"Would you like me to pick you up?" John asked, hoping she would say yes.

Eve appeared conflicted. "I think Mom misses picking me up, and I don't want her to be sad." She briefly paused, trying to come up with an answer that would not hurt her dad's feelings. "I love the time we have been spending together. I am glad you have more time in your schedule to pick me up because we never did fun things together in the past—"

John interrupted his daughter. "Why don't you go back to sleep, and we will talk more tomorrow." This time, John kissed his daughter on the lips, leaving her confused and concerned. Her parents were very demonstrative and loving but never kissed her on her lips before.

John walked into the kitchen and took a beer instead of a glass of water from the fridge before sitting on the sofa in front of the television. "What should I do?" He asked himself several times as he took several sips of beer. He drank one beer after another while he looked at the black television screen for several minutes before going back to his room. John knew he would have to talk to Beverly about his job situation but felt he could get another job and catch up on his bills. He brainstormed until midnight but did not come up with a viable answer to his problem. Another sleepless night staring at the wall while his wife lay beside him, sleeping.

ଔ

Another year passed, and Eve was now a senior in high school. John picked up temporary work that kept the family afloat, but his drinking had gotten out of control. The family continued to struggle and became even more isolated. Eve attended school and worked part-time but missed most of the extra-curricular activities. Instead she spent more time helping her family. Like other girls her age, Eve was interested in attending prom. She dreamed about going to a fancy store and buying a beautiful prom dress but knew the family's financial situation was strained. Unlike other girls her age, she never mentioned having an interest in boys, having a boyfriend, or an interested suiter. She talked about going to college but wanted to stay close to home—perhaps community college. She feared rejection and often avoided social events. Her best friend from junior high had new, socially active friends and spent less time with Eve. She attended a couple events but did not fit in. While the other girls were physically mature, Eve was small and socially awkward. She looked like a thirteen or fourteen-year-old, even though she was seventeen years old.

"Good morning, everyone," Eve announced her arrival in the kitchen. She always had a flair for the dramatic.

"Good morning, honey, how are you doing this morning? Would you like me to pick you up from school today?" Beverly asked her daughter. The family only had one car, and John generally took it to work. "Your dad is going to take the bus today, and I figured we can spend some time together after you get out of school. Maybe we can go shopping after class. What do you think?" It was obvious Beverly was trying to win her daughter's affection and reconnect.

"That's great, Mom. I am excited. I think Dad wanted to pick me up today, but he can pick me up tomorrow." Although Eve was seventeen and could get a driver's license, she continued to depend on her parents to take her to school.

Unwittingly Eve took advantage of the war brewing between her parents for her affection. She reveled in the constant attention but seemed oblivious to the stress that threatened the family's relationship, making it susceptible to fracture. The specter of divorce loomed over John and Beverly Di Angelo. Each turned to their daughter for comfort rather than dealing with the loneliness and pain they experienced. The couple overcompensated by showering their daughter with love and attention in an effort to cover the failure of their relationship. While Beverly struggled with the thought that God did not answer her prayer to save her marriage, John could not face the fact that he was no longer able to provide adequately for the family. The toll it took on the family can best be summarized by the anguish Eve suffered as a result of dysfunctional love.

Although aware of the unconventional and unhealthy relationship her dad had developed with her, Eve did not want to rock the boat. She grappled with the prospect that her dad was turning her into his surrogate wife. Eve loved both parents, but she believed she might hurt their feelings and break up the family if she disclosed what her father was doing. "I think Dad is going through a tough time," she said to Casper, her dog, as she prepared for school. "What do you think I should do? Do you think what Dad did was wrong?" She paused and took a long look in the mirror before making the next statement. "He said that he loves me." Confused by John's love,

Eve constantly made excuses for his behavior. Although she never saw herself as a victim, she knew something was not right. "Casper, we have to help the family stay together. Isn't that what family does?" she asked Casper as she gazed at herself in the long mirror behind the door. The family's practice of don't talk, don't feel, don't tell reinforced Eve's silence and contributed to her emotional conflict.

The Di Angelo's attempts to protect their daughter not only isolated her but promoted a naïveté that kept her from seeing that she was being victimized by her father. Like her parents, Eve learned to ignore her pain and create a make-believe world in which everything and everyone was okay. She had parents who loved her and protected her. "What more can any child need?" she asked herself when she felt sad or worried.

Eve reflected on her mom's excitement about picking her up after school. She also thought about the fact that her dad wanted to spend time with her. "What should I do?" She was keenly aware that the desire to please both parents pulled her in different directions; pleasing them threatened to split her in two. What Eve did not realize was love does not divide, it multiplies. "Dad, I think Mom is going to pick me up today because we are going shopping after school," Eve said tentatively.

John didn't say much. He tried to hide his disappointment behind a smile as he gave Eve a high five. "Okay, honey, you girls have fun." He kissed his daughter and his wife before leaving for work.

"Have fun at work, Dad. Mom and I will certainly have fun shopping," Eve replied to her dad with the childlike glee she was known for.

"Have a nice day at work, honey," Beverly said, unaware that her husband was fired from his full-time job almost a year ago and had been taking on temporary work. John spent most of his off time in a bar downtown before picking Eve up after school. This was the second job John lost in three years. His wife missed most of the signs because he paid the bills with his savings. John borrowed from Peter to pay Paul and struggled to keep the household finances straight. Since his latest dismissal from work, John's life seemed to spiral out of control. His thoughts became increasingly negative and filled with despair. John began drinking to deal with the feelings of helplessness and hopelessness that gradually took over. To add insult to injury, John had sworn Eve to secrecy about the situation.

Lonely and unwilling to talk to his wife about his status on the job, John turned to his teenage daughter for solace and companionship. He often took Eve on outings to get ice cream or on long walks by the beach where they enjoyed watching the waves crash on the rocks. John sometimes discussed his feelings with Eve who became his sounding board and a surrogate wife in a very inappropriate relationship. John deceived himself into thinking that he wasn't doing anything wrong because he only kissed his daughter once or twice but did nothing else. He refused to accept responsibility for the emotional pain he caused his daughter. Instead he selfishly focused on the fact that he was under a lot of stress.

John's role as the primary provider became stressful when he lost his job. Although Beverly worked part-time and had the education to get a better paying full-time job, the couple decided early on that John would be the primary breadwinner. His inability to provide for his family and unwillingness to share the burden with his wife created an invisible wall that both emotionally separated him from Beverly and barricaded him beyond the reach of others. Moreover, he allowed his pain to become a weapon that harmed his family (especially Eve).

"Bye, Mom." Eve walked out the door to catch the school bus right after her father left for work. She smiled from ear to ear as she kissed her mom on the cheek and reminded her to pick her up around 3:00 p.m.

"I wouldn't forget to pick you up. I am looking forward to our girl's evening." Beverly spent the morning cleaning the house and thinking about how fast her little girl had grown up, unaware of the burdensome secret her daughter held and the pain it caused her. Beverly continued to treat Eve like a child, although it was obvious she was becoming a woman. She spent the day thinking about how fast time had flown. "I need to spend more time with my little girl before she goes off to college." She dreamt of her daughter's graduation and first day of college but was not emotionally ready for the separation. "Oh no, I can't believe it is 1:30." Beverly realized that it was getting late. "I better jump in the shower and get ready." It was not long before Beverly was dressed and ready to head to Eve's school.

"Hello, may I help you?" the receptionist in the front office greeted Beverly.

"Hi, my name is Beverly Di Angelo. I am here to pick up my daughter, Eve. She is a senior." Beverly announced as she walked in to the administrative office, beaming with pride.

"Yes, ma'am, I will send someone to get her. Please have a seat." This was Beverly's first venture outside the apartment in a long time. Besides leaving the apartment to go to church and her part-time job three days a week, she rarely ventured outside.

Not long after Beverly took a seat in the waiting area, she heard Eve's voice. "Hi, Mom. I wasn't expecting you this early."

"Hello, honey, ready to go?" Eve could hardly contain her excitement; she got to leave school early and spend time shopping with her mother. They were both looking forward to spending the day together and reconnecting. Moreover, Beverly missed their long talks and Eve's dependence on her.

Eve giggled as she walked out of the office with her mother. "How was your day?"

"We had a quiz, and I think I got an A."

"Really, I am proud of you, honey."

"How was your day, Mom?"

"I had a great day. I could not wait to pick you up for our outing. I missed spending time with you, but I know you have been spending quality time with your father."

Eve became a little nervous, fearing that her mom might ask about her dad. She managed to pull herself together and let Beverly know that she missed spending time with her. Mom and daughter spent the day shopping after having a bite for lunch. They talked about old times, but Beverly focused on Eve's future. "What do you want to study in college?"

"I don't know yet." Eve seemed evasive, or maybe she just wanted to enjoy the day without making future plans.

Following a fantastic day shopping, eating, and talking about fun stuff, Beverly reluctantly reminded her daughter that their outing was coming to an end. "Let's head home. Your dad should be there by now," Beverly said with a hint of sadness in her voice because the time alone with Eve was ending. It was a rare occasion she spent quality time with her daughter. Eve's schoolwork and spending time with John limited their time together.

"I wish we could spend a little more time shopping," Eve said, perhaps an attempt to stay away from the apartment a little longer. "Why can't we stay?" Eve insisted, knowing that they had to return home at some point. Her mom was pleasantly surprised that Eve wanted to spend more time together. She appreciated the fact that although Eve was a teenager, she still enjoyed spending time with her parents.

"I love you," Beverly said as she reached for Eve. Mother and daughter gave each other a hug before heading home.

"Hello, is anyone home?" Beverly called for John as she opened the door to the apartment.

"Hi, I am in the bedroom," John replied as he walked into the living room to greet his wife and daughter.

"How was your day, John?" Beverly asked but could not wait to talk about the wonderful day she had with Eve.

"The usual, work was okay."

"Hi, Dad. How are you?" Eve chimed in as she hugged her father.

"Are you hungry, John? If you give me a few minutes, I can get something whipped up for dinner."

"Don't worry, hon, I am not hungry. I had something earlier."

"Are you sure?" Beverly asked, concerned that John did not have a healthy meal. It was interesting to watch John and Beverly act lovingly in front of their daughter but struggled to communicate when the bedroom door closed.

John still hid the fact that he was no longer working. He left the house daily, deceiving his wife, making her believe he went to work. John spent a great part of the day looking for a job and following up on leads. He became more despondent as the days went by. The couple's marriage continued to drift apart, and they turned their focus on Eve—their saving grace. She became the glue that kept the family together.

As the couple's marriage deteriorated, John stopped going to bed at the same time as his wife to avoid arguing but also to avoid intimacy. Beverly withdrew and became more depressed and angry. Her thoughts centered on feelings of worthlessness and helplessness. The once-vibrant woman began having trouble getting out of bed or doing normal chores. Unable to get out of bed and make it to work most days, she was eventually fired from her job. Her relationship with Bertha was adversely affected when she stopped returning her calls. Isolated from the outside world, Beverly descended into the dark waters of depression.

John on the other hand turned his affections toward his teenage daughter. He spent more time confiding in Eve who was becoming physically mature but emotionally stagnant. Eve took on more of a parental role, caring for her parents and taking care of the household chores. She became increasingly angry but unable to accept the negative feelings that once lay dormant but now rose closer to the surface. Family dinners became more infrequent—each member of the family had to fend for themselves. Eve missed family talks around the dinner table, mom fixing breakfast in the kitchen, and most importantly, the love the family once showed.

The years passed by quickly, leaving the Di Angelo family stuck in a very unhealthy cycle. Frozen in time, Eve took on the responsibilities of nurturing and caring for her parents without the benefit of emotional maturity or support. She began to slip into a fantasy world created by her vivid imagination. She was often confronted by the dichotomy of the fantasy world she created and the reality of being part of a very dysfunctional family dynamic. Eve played the part of a dutiful daughter who cooked, cleaned, and took care of her parents. She was the loving daughter who placed her parents' needs above her own. She attended school most days, worked a part-time job, and took care of the household. Eve never complained nor talked about the family secret. In fact, she kept the secret close to her heart for many years.

On the other hand, John stopped working all together, and his meager social security check, coupled with Beverly's modest disability check, barely took care of the family's financial needs. Combined with Eve's paycheck, the couple's income was barely enough to pay for the rising cost of living in the city. Eve started attending her mother's church to seek spiritual and emotional support but kept others at arm's length. The dissonance created by Eve's need for emotional support and the fear that others may find out about the family's secret became overwhelming. The push/pull left Eve in a very vulnerable state.

Beverly was a member of the church for many years but became less involved with the congregation as things became more difficult at home. Most people run to church when life becomes difficult. Beverly ran from the church. In fact, she seemed to run from God when she most needed him. Beverly was on many church committees. In earlier years, she could not wait for the church doors to open. Now she kept her heart closed to the church. John, on the other hand, was never involved with the church. He attended occasionally but was not convinced by the teachings. Disconnected from outside support, the Di Angelo family remained hidden behind the wall they created for protection.

Initially, Eve did not allow herself to be completely imprisoned by her parents problems. However, she slowly allowed the degradation of her situation to imprison her mind. She completed a few college courses but never finished. Beleaguered by competing priorities, she simply gave up. Her dreams to attend graduate school were placed on the back burner while the family's needs took center stage. She did not maintain contact with her high school friends nor did she have time to establish new friendships during her short stint in college. Overwhelmed by the pain of keeping the family's secret, Eve withdrew from her best friend and others during her last year in high school. Eve deceived herself by thinking she did not need anyone but her mom and dad. They were enough to take care of her needs. Unfortunately Eve did not recognize the importance of a higher power, friendships, extended family, and an objective ear to get through the tough times.

The isolation initially created by her parents' marital issues and subsequent separation from her friends left Eve in an emotionally vulnerable state. She often dealt with the loneliness by writing stories or watching television. Eve sat on her bed for hours on the weekend, watching romantic movies. She hid behind the stories on television while pretending everything in her life was okay. She created a make-believe relationship, a fantasy career, and the perfect life that filled the void formed by the extreme family dysfunction. It was not long before Eve was no longer able to distinguish between fantasy and reality.

"Eve, what are you doing?" John called out to his now twenty-year-old daughter.

"What do you need, Dad? Are you okay?" John was concerned because he had been calling her for a few seconds, and she did not respond. Eve was very familiar with the routine—John called for her anytime he was in the shower, asking for help getting out of the bathtub. John hurt his back five years earlier causing him to go on permanent disability. He fell at the construction site where he briefly worked after being unemployed for couple of years. "I will be right there, Dad." Eve was becoming increasingly irritated with her dad but continued being the dutiful daughter. She often murmured and complained under her breath or simply talked to Casper.

"Here I am," Eve said as she walked into the bathroom to help her dad. John held on to his daughter's arms as she struggled to get him out the tub. "Are you okay, Dad?" Eve asked, ensuring that her dad did not hurt himself as he got out of the tub.

"You are such a good girl. I love you very much," John, who was already inebriated, said as he tried to kiss his daughter on her lips.

"Dad, please stop," Eve begged her dad as she assisted him out of the tub. She was becoming more agitated and unable to hide her frustration. She blamed both parents for her frustration; she especially blamed her dad for having to keep his secret from Beverly. Each time she was summoned to help him out of the tub or to perform duties clearly reserved for a wife, Eve became angrier and more depressed. Her sullen countenance distorted her beautiful face, making her appear older.

"Dad, please. You are making it more difficult for me to help you get out of the tub. Just lean on me," she said as she helped him walk out of the bathroom.

"Okay, honey," John said before sitting on the edge of the bed to get dressed.

Eve turned and walked out of the room. "I will be back to check on you. Call me if you need my help."

In the adjacent room, Beverly lay in bed, watching television. She was oblivious to what was taking place in the household. Although Beverly might beg to differ, her propensity to bury her head in the sand left her daughter unprotected. Eve sometimes wondered about her mother's inability to see what John was doing. "How can Mom not know what is happening?" Eve often asked herself—a question that fueled the fire raging inside her. The embers from her childhood experience were now flaring up into a mature fire while John and Beverly didn't even smell the smoke.

Beverly no longer slept in the same room as her husband. They rarely saw each other because they seldom ventured out of their rooms. John reorganized a large walk-in closet with a single bed and placed a lock on the door. It became his sleeping quarters. The once-vibrant couple who loved each other and were not afraid to show public displays of affection were strangers in their home. Moreover, their daughter became the liaison between them—a surrogate.

Casper, the family's dog, was Eve's constant companion and faithful confidant. She stopped sharing her feelings with her parents especially her dad. "Hey, Casper, what do you want, buddy? Casper stood by the door, wagging his tale and begging for her affection. "Would you like a treat? You've been a good boy today, so you deserve a treat."

Casper was her best friend and confidant. The pair often sat on the bed to watch the latest drama on TV. Most evenings, Eve lost herself in romantic movies, at times, inserting herself in the plot. "I can't believe she can't see that her husband is cheating. What an idiot" She sometimes yelled at the TV and invited Casper to participate in her outrage. "Casper, even you can see that." Too bad she was unable to see the drama that unfolded before her face; it took a long time before she was able to acknowledge the dysfunction in her own life.

"Eve, can you come here," her dad yelled from the bedroom.

"What do you want, Dad?" Eve yelled back rather than going to see what he wanted. There was a time she would have gotten up and rushed to see what he needed. In recent months, she had become more irritable, and her dad's voice started to sound like fingernails on a chalkboard. "I will be there shortly," she snarled. "Casper, can you believe that John is interrupting our movie?" The once-loving daughter stoked the fires of hate toward her father. She began to refer to her dad by his first name. "Can't stand him," she muttered under her breath.

As soon as she helped him back to his bed, he called for something else. "Honey, can you help me get out of bed? I need to go to the toilet." John's back was injured, but his disability was not severe enough to render him helpless. He took advantage of his daughter and tried to exert more and more control over her.

"Thanks, honey, you are the best daughter." John seemed oblivious to his daughter's pain or how his actions made her feel. He became so self-absorbed and obsessed with his relationship with his daughter that he rarely asked about his wife. His actions and lack of interest in Beverly did not go unnoticed by Eve.

In fact, Eve felt guilty and blamed herself for her parents' problems. *I wish Dad could see the person he has become,* Eve thought to herself as she listened to John. *Why can't he acknowledge how much he is hurting me? He cannot be that blind.*

Frustrated and not wanting to be around John, she made up excuses to get far away from him. "Dad, I am a little tired. I'm going to lay in bed and read. I will put a glass of water on your nightstand so you don't have to get out of bed."

"I wish you would lay here with me until you are ready to go to sleep," John said in a very manipulative tone.

"No, Dad, I want to read a book until I fall asleep. Good night, dad." She kissed him on his forehead and walked out, closing the door behind her.

Before heading to her room, Eve stopped by her mother's bedroom to check on her. Beverly slept soundly because of the medications she was taking for depression. "Good night, Mom," she whispered before closing her mother's bedroom door. "Come on, Casper, let's go to bed." Eve went in her room and closed her door before changing into her nightgown. "Come on, boy, let's snuggle and watch TV. You know, Casper, I am tired of dad calling me to take care of his every need. What would he do if I was not around? Plus he has not been very nice to Mom. What do you think? I knew you would agree with me." Eve's relationship with the dog became her saving grace. She no longer attended church and felt distant from God.

The once-effervescent girl was becoming a recluse who spent most of her time talking to her dog, Casper. She worked part-time and didn't seem interested in getting a better full-time job. Her dreams of becoming a therapist appeared to have vanished amid the gloom that casted a shadow on the tiny apartment. Her thoughts were increasingly more negative as she retreated into her world of fantasy. Eve started having trouble sleeping and developed chronic headaches. Her appetite also suffered and became evident in the drastic weight loss.

"Can you believe that guy?" She looked at Casper, expecting some form of response. "If I were him, I would not go into that dark room." She shared her thoughts with Casper as she rewrote the movie's script in her mind. "Ahhhh." Eve yawned and stretched as she got comfortable on the bed. She was getting tired and could barely keep her eyes open. "The movie is almost over. Let's try to stay up a few more minutes. Can you hang with me, Casper?" She mustered all her energy to stay awake until the end of the movie.

The following morning, Eve got out of bed and sat on the couch in the living room for hours. She did not take a shower, check on her parents, or get something to eat. "Eve, could you please come here," her father called for her assistance. This time, Eve did not respond. She simply sat in a catatonic-like state, staring at the black screen on the TV in the living room. "Eve, where are you?" John called out once again. He got up to see why she was not responding. "Are you okay?"

Eve suddenly snapped out of her fog. "Yes, Dad, what do you need?"

"I have been calling you for a few minutes, didn't you hear me?"

"No, I didn't hear you. I was watching TV."

Confused, her dad scratched his head and paused for a few seconds. "Eve, the television is off. It has been off since I walked out to find you." Eve appeared just as confused as her father but did not say anything.

Beverly walked out of her room for the first time in months. "What's going on? I heard John calling you."

"Nothing, Mom. Do you need me to get you something?"

"No, honey, I am okay, I was worried because I heard your dad call you several times."

"Everything is fine. You guys should go back to your rooms." For the first time, Eve's parents became concerned about their daughter's well-being. They had been so self-involved, neither parent noticed that their daughter lost weight and was looking a bit disheveled.

Eve had become so despondent and sapped of her energy, she stopped taking care of her hygiene. Eventually she stopped going to her part-time job. No one seemed to notice that she stopped coming to work. People at the job saw her as a strange person who did not like to be around her peers. She never participated in office events which was not very unusual for part-time employees. No one in the office knew who Eve was. Her presence was barely noticeable. She worked three days a week filing paperwork. She seldom spoke to anyone in the office other than saying good morning or goodbye when she left.

The telephone rang, and Eve answered. "Hello, is this Eve?" the voice on the other line asked.

"Yes, who is this?"

"This is Mr. Thompson, your supervisor. I was calling to see if you are okay. We have not seen you in the office for a couple of days and wondered if you were planning to come back."

"Hello, Mr. Thompson, I have not been feeling well and have been taking care of my parents. I would have called but was unable to get out of bed for a couple of days."

"I am sorry to hear that, Eve. When do you plan to return to work?"

"I plan to go back next week if that is okay? My mom and dad both depend on me to assist them with activities of daily living."

"Please bring a doctor's note when you come back to work next week."

"I will get a doctor's note and take it in next week. Thank you for checking on me." Eve had no plans to see a doctor; in fact, she did not plan to return to work.

"Who was on the phone?" John walked out of the room when he heard the phone ring.

"It was my boss checking on me." Eve turned around and walked to her room without offering further explanation. She locked the door and began talking to Casper about her current situation. "My boss just called to check on me. I think he likes me." Casper barked as if he was responding to her comment. "You agree with me. Don't tell Dad. He might get upset if he finds out. Casper, do you think I will ever get married? Did you know I have a fiancé? I never told you because I wanted to wait until he proposed. Well, guess what? He proposed. We should be getting married next year." Eve continued talking to Casper as if he understood what she was saying. Her thoughts were becoming less cohesive and more tangential.

"Let me check on Mom." She suddenly got up and walked across the hall to her mother's bedroom. "Hello, Mom, how are you feeling? Do you need me to bring you anything?"

"No, honey, how are you feeling today?"

"I am doing well, Mom. I think I might be getting married next year."

Beverly became alarmed. "What are you saying? You don't even have a boyfriend."

"I have not introduced my fiancé because I wanted to wait until he proposed."

"What fiancé? I didn't know you had a boyfriend," a wide-eyed Beverly asked.

"His name is John, just like Dad. We have been dating for several years, but he wanted me to keep it a secret."

Beverly got out of bed as fast as she could to go to her husband's room. "Mom, what are you doing? I want you to get back in the bed. I don't want you to get upset and sick. Anyway, Dad already knows about him."

Beverly suspected something was wrong but did not want to upset her daughter. "Okay, I will stay in bed, but I need to talk to your father about this fiancé of yours."

Concerned that her mom would find out the truth, Eve became agitated. She walked out the room to get her mother's medicine. Instead, she got some sleeping pills and a glass of juice and gave it to her mom. "Here, Mom, take your medicine."

Soon after her mother took the pills, she fell into a deep sleep. An agitated Eve went to her dad's room and began recounting the same story she told her mom. Her dad became visibly upset, but Eve calmed him down by kissing him on the lips; he reciprocated. John took advantage of his daughter's obvious mental illness rather than getting the psychological help she desperately needed. As John tried to pull her in the bed, Eve snapped out of the dream-like state and began to scream. "Hush, you are going to wake your mother and disturb the neighbors."

"Don't touch me," Eve said emphatically as she walked out of the room.

"Okay, I am sorry," John said as he released her arm. John knew that if he followed his daughter, she would start to scream again, so he left her alone.

Eve walked into her room and began talking to Casper. "Can you believe that John tried to hurt me? What should we do?" Eve continued to escalate as she talked about her earlier encounter with her father. "Casper, I am not going to let him hurt me or you. I will protect us and keep the bad man away from us." The once-hero dad had become the enemy in Eve's eyes—a departure from the relationship they had a few years earlier. In fact, the relationship seemed strong and loving a few months ago.

Eve stayed in her room for the remainder of the night but was unable to sleep. She locked her door and plotted her escape from the tomb as she referred to the tiny apartment. She paced back and forth, stopping from time to time to talk to her dog. "Casper, help me formulate a plan of escape. I think John will come after us if we do nothing. I saw it in his eyes today, the way he looked at me told me that he will harm us soon. You know I am right. He has hurt me for the last time." She repeated over and over as her anger escalated. Eve's conversation with the dog made no sense, or maybe it made a lot of sense.

The walls began closing in on her as she lost sight of reality. "I know, I will put a sleeping pill in his beer. What do you think, Casper?" Without hesitation she went to the kitchen and got a beer from the fridge. She opened the bottle and dropped a couple of her mom's sleeping pills in the bottle before offering it to her dad. "Hi, Dad, I brought you beer. You looked stressed, and I thought it might relax you before going to sleep."

"Thank you, honey, how thoughtful of you."

Eve waited as her dad sipped on the beer and became drowsy. She engaged him in small talk as he drifted off to asleep. "Dad, can you hear me?" Eve checked to ensure John was sleeping before she returned to her room.

The following morning, a sleep-deprived Eve opened her bedroom door and, in a zombie-like trance, walked to the kitchen. She stood in front of the stove for a few seconds. Barefoot, Eve wore a yellow nightgown with small flowers and big curlers in her hair to loosen her natural curls. She carried Casper under her arm which was unusual because she generally left him in the room in the mornings. "Are you hungry, Casper? Are you?" she asked forcefully. Eve appeared agitated and hyper-focused. "I will fix us some breakfast, eggs okay?" she asked the dog.

Her eyes were open, but they appeared lifeless. She seemed to be sleepwalking, yet she managed to avoid walking into the furniture or the big vase perched on a stand near the stove. She stood in the middle of the kitchen for what seemed to be an eternity before taking a seat at the kitchen table with a box of matches in her hand. She lit one match after another and blew it out.

"Casper, the fire is so pretty. Look at the blue and red and yellow colors." Eve stared at the matches for a long time before resting them on the table. She walked over to the gas stove and turned the knob of all four burners to the right. She did not turn them all the way up, just enough to allow the gas to slowly escape. The smell of gas permeated the room and floated into the bedrooms where her parents slept. Overcome by the smell of gas, she changed her mind, walked over to the stove, and turned it off. She sat down again and continued to ramble.

"What is that smell, Casper?"

"I see you."

"I know what you are trying to do."

"Get away from me."

"What do you want from me?"

"Why don't you tell me what you want?"

Eve was visibly shaking, and her eyes darted back and forth like she was looking for someone hiding in the house. Following a brief exchange with unseen forces, she stopped talking and listened in silence. "Shhh, Casper, be quiet." Perhaps she was waiting on a response to her questions. Eve suddenly became calm; her demeanor changed, but she seemed oblivious to what was going on around her. It was obvious she was unaware of the magnitude of what had transpired. The consequences were not immediately apparent.

In the bedroom next to the kitchen, her mom lay in a deep sleep as a result of the medication she took the night before. Her father rested in a make-shift bedroom next to Beverly's room. Unaware of the deadly gas that slowly leaked from the stove into each room, both parents remained in bed. Overcome by the smell of gas and smoke that started to rise in the kitchen, Eve started coughing and decided to open the window. Unfortunately it was too late, the table cloth caught fire when she lit one of the matches and didn't put it out completely before setting it on the table. She did not intend to harm her parents nor did she intend to kill herself, at least not consciously.

Fire, fire, fire. The next-door neighbor saw smoke coming from the apartment and called 911. She ran and knocked on the Di Angelo's door, but no one opened at first. Finally Eve opened the door and walked out in a zombie-like state. She did not say a word. Eve sat motionless near the elevator while others desperately tried to put out the fire before the fire department arrived. Although the fire did not engulf the entire building and no one in the neighboring apartments were hurt, John and Beverly succumbed to the smoke. No one knew they were in the apartment. In a state of shock, Eve did not let the neighbors know that her parents were still inside.

"What happened?" one of the neighbors asked but did not get a response.

"Are you hurt, ma'am?" the young man in an EMS uniform asked as he escorted Eve to the ambulance. Amid the chaos, one of Beverly's church sisters, who lived across the street, offered some information to the police and paramedics.

"I know her. She goes to my church." Eve remained silent and unfettered by the chaos that unfolded around her. Despite police questioning, the presence of neighbors, and the turmoil around her, Eve appeared disconnected from the situation and her surroundings.

"I am Wanda, a friend of the family. We attend the same church, and I know her parents." Wanda offered to accompany Eve to the hospital since she was in no shape to assist paramedics or hospital personnel.

"What's your name?" The admitting nurse asked but did not get a response. Eve seemed to have blacked out.

"Her name is Eve Di Angelo." Wanda volunteered. "She is in her late twenties or early thirties, I am not sure."

"Ma'am, are you a relative?" The nurse asked, cognizant of patient privacy rules.

"I am a neighbor, and we attend the same church. I think Eve's parents were in the apartment, no one knows yet. I don't think Eve has any other relatives in the area. The family kept to themselves and didn't talk about their relatives."

"Eve, could you tell me if you are having any pain?" The nurse once again tried to engage her. "I am going to take your blood pressure, temperature, and pulse, is that okay? By the way, my name is Hope. Let me know if you are uncomfortable in any way."

Eve barely opened her eyes and looked up at the nurse but closed them again. Hope handed Wanda a hospital gown and directed her to change Eve's clothing before she could start an IV. Although Eve appeared to be unconscious, the nurse spoke to her as she rendered aid. "Eve, I am going to give you some fluids because you are a little dehydrated. You will feel an initial pinch but nothing major." Eve did not respond.

Eve kept her eyes closed as Hope explained the admission process and what she could expect every step of the way. She did not speak, open her eyes, or move. She remained in the same position.

Finally I have escaped the tomb, a thought popped in her head, but she could not vocalize it. Eve did not appear to understand what was going on around her. Aside from the shallow breathing, it was hard to tell if she was alive. She didn't even react to the pinch of the IV needle. The fluids coursing through her vein was like an infusion of new life. Although Eve was not responsive to the external world, she entertained a conversation in her mind. *I am alive and free. No longer a watermark on someone's page. Life is not always fair, but its fairness lies in our ability to recognize that we are not alone on this journey.*

Eve, like many of us, searched for the missing piece of the puzzle. The piece that eludes many and sends others on a journey filled with pain. She discovered that in the mist of her pain, there was someone who gave her hope and peace beyond her ability to understand. "Lean not on your understanding. If you believe in God, believe also in me." A voice gave her comfort as she lay on the hospital bed in the emergency room. Eve was finally out of the tomb. The tiny apartment she saw as a tomb buried in the dark, that dark place is also where buried seeds grow into trees that reach the sky. The missing piece of the puzzle was always inside her. She did not recognize it because of the darkness that surrounded her.

If you feel like you are in a dark place, perhaps you are buried like a seed so you may grow into a tree. Some people feel physically trapped, others are emotionally stuck. There is a spiritual freedom available for you. The missing piece of the puzzle unlocks the tomb. Although John was the source of a lot of Eve's pain, there is another John that holds the key or maybe the missing piece of the puzzle. Read John 3:16, you will find the missing piece. "For God so loved the world that he gave his one and only son, that whoever believes in him shall not perish but have eternal life (NIV)."

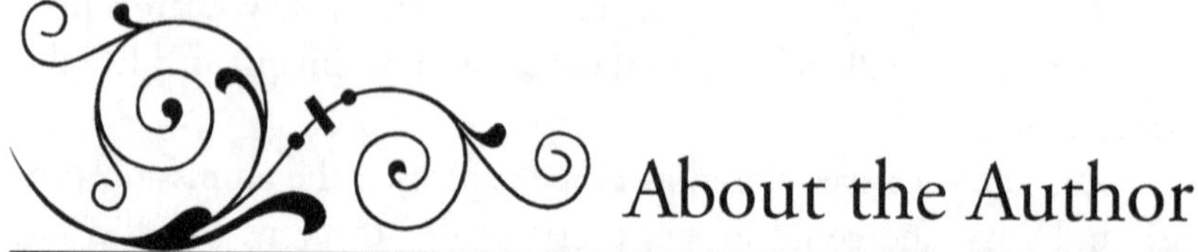

About the Author

Dr. Nola Veazie is a licensed therapist and certified drug and alcohol counselor who spent over twenty years in the US Air Force. She started women's support groups that helped hundreds of active duty and civilian women overcome challenges. Following retirement, she started V-Solutions Consulting, LLC, a service-disabled, veteran-owned small business that provides training and consulting services to a number of organizations.

CPSIA information can be obtained
at www.ICGtesting.com
Printed in the USA
BVHW071444071019
560429BV00003B/250/P